TO KISS A KING

REGENCY ROYALS BOOK 4

JESS MICHAELS

For Michael. You're the one I wanted, want now want when I am old. Manchester Orchestra sums it up perfectly.

AUTHOR'S NOTE

There are a lot of conversations about the concept of Content Warnings in books and for other media. Having suffered from panic attacks that were triggered by trauma, I would NEVER wish that on my worst enemy. I want you to enjoy what you're reading, never be pulled away because you were surprised by triggering material. So, I will do my best to include Content Warnings in an author note in each book from now on. Also, look to my website for them, so that you don't accidentally buy a book that might give you pause.

Content Warning: childhood physical and emotional abuse (described/not on page), physical assault

PROLOGUE

Spring 1817
London

"**I** cannot believe we shall meet a king!" Ophelia said, grasping her sister-in-law Abigail's arm with both hands. "How thrilling!"

Abigail smiled as Ophelia twisted a few of her curls a bit more artfully around her cheeks and smoothed her gown. "Thanks to your brother's position, you have met a great many important people of rank and position."

Ophelia shrugged. "I suppose so. Though I'm not sure I would compare any of those ancient bores to the King of Athawick." She waggled her eyebrows playfully. "You cannot pretend you haven't heard the stories. Seen the artist renderings of the man in the papers."

Abigail shot her a look. "You are talking about how handsome he is supposed to be?"

"A king who isn't ancient or gouty," Ophelia breathed. "Imagine that. And we are to meet him before the arrival ball. Practically the moment he has disembarked from the ship from Athawick."

"It does speak highly of your brother that our family was chosen as one of the few who will have this brief private audience before the ball, yes."

Ophelia nodded. Of course, she wouldn't expect any less. Her brother, Abigail's husband, was the Duke of Gilmore. And no better a man or duke would one find in all of England, Ophelia would have strong words with anyone who debated her on that topic.

"Now what is *that* look?" Abigail asked, reaching out to take Ophelia's hand gently.

Ophelia ducked her head. Though the new duchess had not been in their family very long, she and Ophelia were already as close as sisters could be. And there was no hiding from her sharp observations. "I was just thinking how very different Nathan and I are. And hoping he won't regret including me in tonight's festivities."

Abigail's expression softened. "Nathan would never regret bringing you anywhere. And you two are not so very different. Oh, he plays the very serious duke in public, of course. It is how he is expected to behave. But you know as well as I do that he can be open and warm and funny in private, just as you are."

"Wild," Ophelia said softly. "He once described me as wild."

Abigail flinched slightly at that assessment, and Ophelia immediately wished she had not brought up the topic. It was of specific pain to Abigail, and Ophelia would not ever cause her pain on purpose.

"My dearest, you are sunshine and brightness and everything lovely," Abigail said. "You bring enthusiasm and fun into every room you enter. And if you sometimes go a...a bit too far...well...your captivating nature will always offer you more forgiveness than censure on that score, I think. Especially since I have never known you not to have the best interest of everyone you meet at heart. In that way, you and your brother are very much alike. And I love you both for that charming and wonderful quality."

Ophelia wrapped her arms around Abigail and squeezed gently. "As we both adore you."

She stepped back, blinking at tears that had suddenly leapt into her eyes. She grabbed Abigail's arm and tugged her to the mirror against the wall in her dressing chamber. Together they stood, looking at the image of themselves in the glass.

Abigail was beautiful in a dark pink gown with lighter highlights through the pleating on her skirt. And Ophelia had had a new gown made for this very occasion, a creamy silk adorned with peacock feather ornamentation in the flow of the skirt and a line of folded and braided silks along the apex. She wore a pale purple silk robe over it, with more peacock highlights on the shoulders and pleating so it fell just perfectly. Her maid had tucked and curled and pinned her hair with jeweled clips.

"Look at us," Ophelia teased. "There will be no resisting either one of us—this handsome king will surely fall madly in love and it will be a passionate scandal."

Abigail burst out in laughter, shaking her head. "You are outrageous. I promise he will not fall in love with me. And no one could resist falling in love with you. Now come, we are expected shortly and must make our way."

Ophelia laughed as they made their way downstairs and were greeted by her brother. Nathan's eyes lit up when he saw Abigail, and there was almost an audible hum between them as they met and he kissed her quite shamelessly right there in the foyer. Ophelia was very happy for them. She just wished she didn't feel a slightly darker emotion, as well. One she shoved aside as they crowded into the carriage.

It was a lively trip to the royal residence where the Athawickians were staying during their Season in London. Bleaking House was beautiful and Ophelia was properly impressed as they were helped from the carriage and into the home, itself. The butler took them to a formal parlor, one with dour portraits of past English royals hanging from every wall, staring down at them as they waited for the arrival of their host.

Ophelia stepped away from the others, moving to the fire to

look at the miniatures placed there. She shook her head. A little porcelain shepherdess and her sheep. The vapid look that had been captured in the piece was really quite something.

She pivoted to say something about it to her brother and Abigail when the door opened and the butler who had escorted them stepped back inside. "His Royal Majesty, King Grantham of Athawick."

He stepped aside, bowing his head low as a tall man made his way into the chamber. Ophelia was vaguely aware that her brother had bowed and Abigail curtseyed, and yet all she could do was stand there, staring at the king.

However he had been described either in official stories in the papers or by breathless ladies in drawing rooms, he far exceeded all expectation. He had dark hair, cut close, which only served to high-light an angular face below it. He wore a well-trimmed beard, thwarting the style of the day in London. But he wore it so well, it didn't matter. She would guess every man in the city would be wearing a beard before year's end to copy him. But not a one of them would capture the dark, focused look of him. The fullness of his lips, the way he moved as he entered a room.

He had dark eyes that flitted across the room with a sort of prac-ticed boredom. They moved over the others and then slid to her. He held her gaze for a beat, another, and she realized she wasn't breath-ing. She didn't remember *how* to breathe, truth be told.

Then his lips pinched, and his nostrils flared. He turned his gaze away and she realized he was...*dismissing* her.

"The Duke and Duchess of Gilmore, Your Majesty," said a tall, thin man who had entered the room silently behind the king.

"Good evening, Your Graces," the king said, motioning her brother and Abigail forward.

"Your Majesty," Nathan said, and he and Abigail bowed and curt-seyed a second time. "And may I present my younger sister, Lady Ophelia."

Ophelia somehow found the use of her legs and made her way

across the room to stand before the king. Good gracious he was tall. "Your Majesty," she managed to squeak out. Abigail gently nudged her with her elbow and Ophelia started. Oh yes, the curtseying. She managed to execute a swift one, and again the king's gaze narrowed on her.

"How are you enjoying London, Your Majesty?" Nathan asked. "As much as you have seen of it in a few short hours."

"I fear the family has not yet been able to take in all that the city has to offer," the king admitted. "Although I have been here before, of course, for a year of my education and also during official visits over the years before my father's death."

"And what do you think of our fair city?" Ophelia found herself asking.

His gaze moved to her again and now the brow wrinkled. "It is fine, my lady." He turned away to her brother. "Your Grace, I have heard that you have begun investing in some shipping endeavors that may affect my country. I assume the ladies would not mind if we took a moment to discuss the future of our mutual interests."

He didn't wait for either Abigail or Ophelia to respond, but motioned Nathan away. When he was gone, Ophelia crossed her arms. "What an unpleasant man."

Abigail jerked her gaze to Ophelia. "You think so?"

"He was very dismissive, didn't you think?"

"I think he's serious and focused," Abigail said. "A bit like your brother, actually. But I didn't feel he was particularly unpleasant. He is certainly as handsome as the papers and gossips have said over the last few breathless weeks."

Ophelia pursed her lips. He was that, there was no denying it. Even now she couldn't keep her eyes off the man as he stood over by the window, firelight dancing over his harsh features and seeming to highlight each one.

He glanced her way and she jolted, hating that her cheeks heated as she pivoted so she would no longer face him.

"Well, handsome or not, king or not, I don't like him," Ophelia said softly.

Abigail gave her a confused look, but shrugged. "Then it is likely a good thing that the king and his family will be very busy during this trip. There is no reason why you would have to spend an inordinate amount of time with him."

Ophelia smoothed her hands along her skirt and nodded, even as she looked over her shoulder at him one more time. "Yes. A very good thing."

CHAPTER 1

A few months later

Grantham, King of Athawick, sat at the desk a dozen kings had sat at before him, staring at the notes from the blue box that had been delivered an hour before. The same box was left on his desk at the same time every morning, brimming with reports from each member of his cabinet, the head of his navy and his courtiers. Missives for a king so that he would be better able to keep track of his kingdom.

Over the centuries, there had been kings in his line who had all but ignored the box. Always to their detriment and the detriment of their people. But Grantham's father, Alistair, the previous king of Athawick, had been many things—most of them unpleasant—but he had driven into Grantham the importance of duty.

And so Grantham glanced over the papers once more, lips pursing at the reports therein. Things were...*complicated* in his kingdom.

There was a light knock on his study door. Without looking up, he called out, "Enter."

"Hard at work, I see."

He glanced up now and saw that his brother, Prince Remington, had entered the study. Although raised in the same family, sometimes Grantham thought they had to be different species. After all, Remi was light and fun and effortless. Grantham could be none of those things. And while it often got his brother in trouble, he'd always been a little jealous of Remi's untethered enthusiasm and excitement.

"I was hard at work," Grantham said.

Remi tilted his head. "I shall not keep you, I only came to ask you a certain question."

Grantham sighed. "I have already given permission for the wedding in four days, Remi. If there is anything else on that score, I would suggest you take it up with the queen. Mother is handling everything else."

Remi beamed at that statement and the twinge of jealousy Grantham had been trying to tamp down rose up again, this time louder and stronger. Somehow his wayward brother had managed to fall head over heels in love with one of the recent visitors to their island, an Englishwoman named Priscilla who had come with some family friends to attend their younger sister's wedding.

Christ, it was as if chaos had been his constant companion lately. Grantham loathed chaos.

"It isn't about the wedding. Priscilla and I have that well in hand," Remi said, and there was such a pure joy on his face that Grantham had to stare. "The request is something else."

Grantham set his pen down and leaned back in his chair. "Very well then, what is it?"

"It's about Lady Ophelia."

For a moment everything in Grantham's world seemed to stop. His brother's voice still droned, but it sounded like Remi was in a bubble somewhere far away.

Lady Ophelia. There was one of those chaotic topics he wished to avoid and yet never seemed to be able to do so. The woman was the sister of the Duke of Gilmore, an important guest and someone Grantham might call a friend after the past few months.

She, on the other hand, was something else entirely. She was the kind of woman who entered a room and made the world tilt. Someone who laughed too loud and too often. She danced and spun and teased and made it impossible not to look at her.

She was, in short, a hoyden, and Grantham had been doing his level best to avoid her both in London and Athawick. And yet she was always there, drawing his attention. Making him feel the strangest stirrings in his stomach, making him dream of her.

He blinked, for he realized Remi was still speaking.

"—and because of that, Priscilla would love to have Ophelia here for the wedding. So I'm asking your permission that she might stay a few weeks longer."

Grantham pushed to his feet, turning away and hoping his brother would not be able to hear the heart that had begun to pound out of his chest. Christ, he had always had control over himself before, why could he not find it now?

"You want Lady Ophelia and the rest of the Gilmore party to stay?" he managed to say.

Remi hesitated. "Er, no. As I said, because the Duke of Gilmore has promised to return Priscilla's horrible parents back to London and keep them from destroying her, he cannot stay. And I think the duchess would not wish to be parted from him for weeks upon weeks."

Grantham pivoted. "You wish Lady Ophelia to stay on Athawick unchaperoned?"

Remi's eyes went wide at the sharpness of Grantham's tone. "She would not exactly be unchaperoned, though. Priscilla would look after her—"

"Oh yes, I'm sure she will make that a priority when she isn't sneaking into your room or the tower with you every night."

Remi broke into a wide grin. "I am utterly ruining her, I know.

Or perhaps she is doing the ruining. Certainly I am not the man I once was and I do not miss him."

Grantham's expression softened despite the topic. No, Remi wasn't the same. He was changed by love, just as their two sisters Ilaria and Sasha had been equally changed in the last few months as they met and married the loves of their lives. He was the only sibling left who had not found his heart's desire.

And he was in no position to lament that fact. He had no time for such emotions. Even if he did, he would have to make a political alliance, not one for his heart. And he couldn't think of that until after he resolved Athawick's other issues.

"At any rate," Remi continued, "Mama will surely be happy to play chaperone. And Ophelia has her lady's maid present. She is not a child—she won't go running wild."

"No, she is not a child, but I wouldn't count on the second thing," Grantham grumbled. "She always seems one tumbler of strong punch away from…from…"

"From what?" Remi asked, tilting his head. "I would love to know how you would finish that sentence."

Grantham knew exactly how he might finish that sentence. In a half dozen incredibly inappropriate scenarios that he shoved from his mind as he refocused his energy and smoothed his jacket with both hands.

"This is what Priscilla wishes?" he asked softly.

Remi nodded. "Very much so."

Grantham sighed. "My future sister has been through a great deal during her time with us. I would never deny her something that would make her happy. You may tell her to ask Lady Ophelia."

Remi's expression lit up, and for a moment all Grantham could think about was racing along the beach with his brother when they were boys, before their lives had become so complicated. Before walls had been erected between them that felt so impossible to climb.

"Thank you," Remi said, and it seemed entirely sincere. "I will do so straight away. See you tonight, yes?"

"Of course. Where else would I be?" Grantham grumbled, returning to the window as his brother rushed from the room. His study overlooked the garden and down below he saw that Ophelia, herself, had stepped out with the Duchess of Gilmore and Priscilla. The women were talking and laughing, but the most animated of all was Ophelia.

His entire body felt like it clenched, even more so when she glanced up toward the study window. She could see him there, he was certain. He had stood in that very place in the garden many a time and looked up to see his own father watching.

And just like his face had done all those times, her expression fell, her smile fading. He backed away and returned to his desk where he sat, wishing his mind wasn't racing, trying to get himself back into focus.

Before he could, there was another knock on the door and he looked up to find his head courtier, Stephen Blairford, entering the room, a pile of papers in his hand.

Blairford was older than him by at least twenty years. He had served Grantham's father and it was expected that he would carry on in his role as head courtier. Grantham had always felt uneasy about him, truth be told, and even more so as of late. But the man knew everything, and with the island in such upheaval, it was hard to turn help away.

"Good morning, Your Majesty," he said with a small bow. When he straightened his mouth was pinched.

"What is the problem, Blairford?" Grantham asked. He felt the tension in his body shift, thoughts of Ophelia fading slightly.

His courtier cleared his throat. "There were more of those fliers left tacked to the gate this morning," Blairford said. *"Freedom for Athawick.* With the reverse flag."

Grantham pressed his lips together. There was the problem with his kingdom. It seemed some didn't want it to be his anymore. "They were removed?" he asked softly.

"Yes, and burned," Blairford said. "They are becoming bolder to place them right on the gate."

"They want to be heard," Grantham mused, and ran a hand through his hair. He nudged his head toward the stack of papers. "Are those for me to sign?"

Blairford nodded and laid out the papers along Grantham's desk, and as they began to talk about what had been placed before him, he sighed. *This* was what he needed to focus on now: his country. He couldn't let an English sprite keep him from his duty.

~

Ophelia stared up at the window where she had seen King Grantham standing a fraction of a moment before. Staring at her. Frowning at her.

She shivered. Normally she was certain of herself, at least mostly. But the man threw her off every time she looked at him. He made her hot and cold all at once, made her brain rush with thoughts that were entirely inappropriate. She knew he didn't like her, his expression made it abundantly clear every time he looked at her. Not that he seemed to *like* anyone. He was too grumpy a person for something so frivolous as affection.

"Oh, look," Priscilla said, her entire countenance lighting up. "Here comes Remi."

Ophelia pushed away her thoughts and glanced back at the steps leading from the terrace high above. Prince Remi was, indeed, coming down the stairs, a broad smile on his handsome face. Priscilla practically bounced as he neared them, the joy glowing from deep within her.

Abigail gave Ophelia a quick look and the two women stepped back to allow the soon-to-be-married lovers to reunite. Although they'd seen each other at breakfast, the way Priscilla took his hand, the way he leaned into her, one might have thought it had been days.

He whispered something to Priscilla, and her friend's smile grew as she linked her arm through his and the two moved to her and Abigail.

"It is done," he said, nodding to Abigail.

Ophelia cocked her head. "Done? What is done? Are you three concocting plans and daring to leave me out of them? Badly done!" she teased.

Priscilla laughed. "We were doing just that, but out of nothing but the best reasons, I assure you. We only wanted to be certain before we spoke to you. And now it has all come to fruition."

Ophelia wrinkled her brow. "Since Pris insists on speaking in riddles, perhaps you would like to explain, Your Highness."

Remi chuckled. "Indeed. As you well know, I would do anything to make my future wife happy, and one thing would make her very much so. That is for you, Ophelia, to stay in Athawick for our wedding and a few weeks longer after that."

Ophelia blinked, watching Priscilla nod with enthusiasm and Abigail beam with pleasure on her behalf. She felt very little of it herself. She had begun to count the days to her return to London, count the days until she would no longer be under the watchful and judgmental eye of the King of Athawick.

"I…" she began. "Surely the king and queen must be looking forward to having the privacy of the palace back after the guests these past few weeks."

"The king is very pleased to have you stay," Remi said. "He was just telling me before I came down to inform you of the invitation."

Her stomach flipped at the idea that Grantham…King Grantham had been talking about her. Remi might make it sound pleasant and friendly, but she knew better, didn't she? There was no way the king was pleased about anything at all, certainly not her.

She turned her attention to Abigail. "You and Nathan would need to discuss this, I think, before I could answer."

Abigail beamed. "We already have, my dear. The royal family has kindly agreed to act as chaperone. There is nothing holding you back from staying and enjoying the extra time on this beautiful island."

"So you…you would not stay."

Abigail glanced toward Priscilla. "We have our escort duties to perform."

Ophelia shook her head. Of course they did. She was being selfish to forget. Priscilla's father and her horrible stepmother had showed up unexpectedly on the island only days ago, creating all kinds of stress and pain for her friend. Nathan and Abigail were marching them home, and that was a very important duty to protect Priscilla.

She glanced apologetically at her friend and was happy to see that Remi had put his arm around her, his expression growing dark momentarily. He truly did love her. He would do anything to protect her. And so would Ophelia.

Priscilla stepped forward and took her hands. "The wedding is private, of course. Only family. And there is no one else in the world that I could call family but you. Please won't you stand up for me, Ophelia?"

Ophelia blinked back sudden tears at the question. One she could never say no to. "Of course I will," she said, embracing her friend tightly. "I would move heaven and earth for your happiness, if you wish this, I wouldn't miss it."

"Wonderful!" Remi said. "And without so many guests around, you'll get to truly enjoy the palace and the island, and get to know my family all the better."

Ophelia nodded and forced a smile, but there was the rub, wasn't it? With a household full of guests, with her brother and Abigail and Priscilla as buffers, she had been able to avoid too much private contact with King Grantham. And yet being around him was still difficult.

What would it be like with all those buffers gone? With nothing between them to keep his disdain from being plain? He would not hide it, after all. She always felt his regard, hot at her back, seeping through her skin and into her blood. Sometimes he almost drew her in with long looks.

But when he turned away, it was almost always with a look of disgust. And if he knew her past? What she was? What she'd done?

Certainly he would feel even more of the same.

But staying here wasn't about him, was it? It was about Priscilla, who she considered a sister. And she would not allow the cantankerous King of Athawick to ruin her last lovely days with her best friend.

She would just have to find a way to ward him off. Or make him accept her. Either way, it would only be a few weeks longer.

CHAPTER 2

The past few weeks on Athawick had been filled with swirling balls to celebrate the recent nuptials of Princess Ilaria and her handsome Captain Crawford. They had begun to blend together for Ophelia, and yet tonight felt…different as she stared out over the crowd that was bobbing about in a happy Athawickian folk dance. The faces were the same as they had ever been. The gowns were as beautiful and the music as wonderful. The gentlemen were on the hunt, the ladies pretending to be helpless prey, just as was true in any ballroom.

But something had definitely changed. At least for her. Perhaps because it was the last ball of this event. In the morning the ship back to London would fill with all these faces and all would sail into the horizon. All but her.

She sighed and turned to move away from the crowd. Only to find herself nearly careening into the broad chest of King Grantham. She hadn't even heard him approach and she staggered back with a gasp.

"You—Your Majesty," she said when she could find her breath. She offered a quick curtsey. "Good evening."

"Lady Ophelia," he said, drawing out her name ever so slightly.

He then said nothing else, but simply stepped up beside her, and together they watched the dancing crowd a moment. She shifted under the weight of the silence. The man was an expert at it, that was certain. Also at staring.

She cleared her throat when she could take it no longer. "I-I wished to say thank you for your kindness."

He glanced at her. "My kindness?"

"In allowing me to stay for Prince Remington and Priscilla's wedding."

He grunted rather than answered and returned his attention to the ball. She waited a moment and then added, "You must wish to have your palace back from interlopers."

He grunted again, though that particular sound felt more in the affirmative.

She pursed her lips. Great God, but the man was frustrating. Why had he approached her, why was he standing next to her if he was only going to be so taciturn and uncommunicative? Was he just playing a game with her?

She blinked and looked at him from the corner of her eye. Perhaps she was right. Perhaps this man just liked to watch her squirm. The more she mulled over that in her mind, the more sense it made. From the very first time she met him he had been...*odd* in her presence. Watching her even as he avoided her.

Was it all a game to him?

Well, if that were true, she could certainly play it. Match his energy with her own opposite one. If he wanted to be gruff and untalkative, she could be fluffy and light and playful and chatty, couldn't she? Take the upper hand by batting her eyelashes at him and driving him mad?

It might actually make the next few weeks bearable. She smothered a laugh and turned to face him directly. His expression fluttered when she did, as if she had surprised him. Good.

"Your Majesty, I simply *must* compliment you on your gardens. Every morning I take a long walk and they are truly stunning. It's clear the generations of work that have gone into the blooms. I, myself, have a rather black thumb, I fear. I cannot even manage to keep a bouquet alive for more than twenty-four hours. Perhaps that's a curse." She paused only for a quick breath and continued, loving how his eyes were progressively growing wider as she chattered on. "Not that I believe in such a thing as a curse. I'm far more reasonable a person than that. It's all science, isn't it? Water a plant well and it will grow. Give it food and sunlight and I suppose I'm simply not focused enough to recall to do it. Not that I'm flighty. Heavens, no."

His mouth was dropped just slightly open and his gaze was entirely focused on her now. No, wait, not on her. On her mouth. As if he was trying to figure out how it was pushing so many words out at once. Excellent.

She drew a deep breath and continued, "I noted that Princess Ilaria's bouquet was from the garden. What a wonderful wedding that was. They seem truly in love, as do Princess Sasha and the Earl of Bramwell. And of course our dear Priscilla and Remi. Love matches seem to be as in fashion in Athawick as they are presently in London. What do you think of that, Your Majesty?"

He opened and shut his mouth several times and then cleared his throat. "I think that I wish to see my family happy," he said slowly. "And they are. So that is good enough for me."

She was actually taken aback by that response. She had never been able to read the king's response to the flurry of romances and marriages amongst his siblings in the past few months. But what he said seemed...genuine.

"My lady, would you like to dance?" he asked.

She caught her breath. They had known each other for months, been present at dozens of these events both at home and here in Athawick, and yet he had never requested a dance with her. He'd danced with Priscilla, with Abigail...but never her.

"I..." she murmured, and then shook her head. This was surely still part of his game…or if he wasn't playing one, she needed to incorporate it into her own.

"Yes," she said. "That would be an honor, Your Majesty."

"Excellent," he said, motioning her toward the floor, where the previous country jig had ended and couples were filtering on and off. She thought she heard him mutter something else as he followed her. Something about the only way to make her stop talking.

She smothered a smile. Excellent. If they were to be adversaries, she intended to win the day. And flummoxing him was fun. Certainly more entertaining than the time she'd spent avoiding him and wondering why he wouldn't stop looking at her.

As they reached the center of the ballroom floor, she realized the room had turned to watch them. The other dancers stepped back a fraction, leaving them space. Of course they would. The king was dancing. No one wanted to miss that.

He let out his breath slightly and met her gaze as he reached out to take her hand. She caught her own breath when he did so. This was the first time he had ever touched her. She realized it in a heady moment of dizzy recognition. Even through both their gloves, she felt the heat and weight of his fingers as he glided them around her hand.

When he put the opposite hand on her waist, she stopped breathing entirely, staring up into dark eyes that locked with her own. He was very close now. Too close and not close enough all at once.

"I think you are meant to touch my shoulder, Lady Ophelia," he said softly, his voice rough. "And then we must move eventually."

She blinked as she realized the first notes of the waltz had, indeed, already begun. She swiftly lifted her hand to his shoulder and ignored the ripple of muscle that followed as she did so. He stepped out, guiding her with no effort, a graceful gliding of feet and body.

There was such confidence in every step, and she found herself entirely trusting him to guide her. Oh, a man was always meant to lead in the dance, but that didn't mean a lady shouldn't protect herself on the floor. Half the men she'd danced with had careened her into others or stepped on her feet. She had to lead sometimes without looking like she was doing so.

But not with this man.

He said nothing as he maneuvered her. Not even a pleasantry. And since she felt entirely stunned into her own silence, his expression returned to the usual one he wore when he was around her. Unreadable except for flashes of what she had to believe was dislike.

He didn't like her. She had known that from the first moment they met. And she didn't need every person she met to like her. She had more than enough friends in her life. But even as she believed he didn't feel anything for her but negativity, she also felt the draw of him. The tug of his gaze as he moved her around the floor. The flutter of…

Well, she would not label that flutter. She knew what it was. She'd felt it before, much to her own detriment and the pain of a great many others. That flutter would lead to nothing good. And in this case, it was entirely confusing.

A few more turns around the floor and the music faded. He released her waist so that she might execute a curtsey and he followed with a bow. Then he tucked her hand into the crook of his elbow and led her to the edge of the dancefloor. He released her and stood, still staring at her for a long moment.

Then he inclined his head. "Good evening, my lady."

"G-Good evening," she whispered back as he pivoted and walked away from her. He cast no look back—he just made his way through the crowd until he disappeared from view.

There was a light touch on her arm and she jumped as she pivoted to face whomever had approached. It was Priscilla, who had an odd look on her face. Concern mixed with…something else. Recognition of some kind, like she'd just solved a riddle.

"Good evening," Ophelia said, and was surprised to find herself breathless. She forced a bright smile. "You look beautiful, of course."

"As do you," Priscilla said slowly. "Would you...would you like to take a turn on the terrace and talk to me about anything?"

Ophelia shifted. "I don't know what you think I would like to talk about, but if you have something on your mind, I'm at your service, of course."

She found herself glancing over her shoulder, but she did not find Grantham.

"Ophelia," Priscilla said, this time more firmly.

Ophelia looked back at her. "What is it, dearest? You seem so concerned."

"I suddenly *am* concerned," Priscilla said. "You and the king—"

Ophelia raised a hand, not wanting Priscilla to continue that line of questioning at present. "Are just as we always have been. He thinks me foolish, I think him cold and unfeeling. It matters little. There are only a few weeks left in our acquaintance and then I shall rarely see him again."

At that Priscilla's expression crumpled slightly. "Or...or me."

Ophelia swallowed hard. She'd been trying to avoid that subject as well. "Yes," she whispered. "Of course that is a very sad fact. You will be in Athawick living the most wonderful happily ever after that will be better than any fairytale."

"I hope so. Fairytales can be ghastly things." Priscilla smiled, though there were tears in her eyes. "And I'm being maudlin, of course. I will come to London regularly, as I know Remi will wish to see his sisters. And you will come here."

Ophelia nodded. "I shall, if you like. If the king will give his permission."

She could see that inspired Priscilla to want to broach the subject of Grantham again, so she caught her friend's hands in hers and laughed. "But since we only have a few weeks left in this visit, I propose that you and I dance."

Priscilla let out a peal of laughter as Ophelia dragged her onto the dance floor and into the middle of the lively jig that was being performed by the others. Her action did as she had hoped. It eased some of the sadness between them...and it utterly distracted Priscilla from whatever she had wanted to say about Grantham. About the dance that still confused Ophelia and made her stomach flutter in ways it ought not.

Ways it never could again. Confounding the man was one thing...but that...*that* was something else entirely.

G rantham could not take his eyes off of Ophelia as she spun about the dancefloor, hands clasped in Priscilla's, head tilted back with joyful laughter. Of course, he had long determined the impossibility of taking his eyes off the woman at all.

Dancing with her had only made it worse. Solidified the very problem he had been trying to avoid: He wanted her.

He had wanted her from the first moment he walked into the parlor at Bleaking House and saw her standing at the fireplace with an expression of pure mischief on her beautiful face. How small his world had shrunk in that moment. How odd that he had been permanently changed by something so simple.

It was infuriating, really.

Of course, he was not the only one who watched her. The entire crowd did so at present, clapping along to the music, following Ophelia with their eyes. Like she was summer and everyone in the room wanted to be closer to the sun.

"How are you, dearest?"

Grantham turned slightly as his mother stepped up beside him, sliding her arm through his and giving a gentle squeeze.

"Fine as one can be, considering," he answered, returning his attention to the dancefloor. The song had ended and Priscilla and Ophelia were making an enormous show of their bows to each other at the end. The crowd applauded their entertainment as they giggled off together toward where Remi stood, beaming without hesitation at it all.

Of course he could. He was free to be so much more than Grantham could hope for. In that moment, the jealousy was intense.

His mother took his hand, drawing his attention back to her. "I would love to…to talk to you, my love. To help you if I can. Will you talk to me? Talk to Dash?"

Grantham looked off into the distance a moment. His mother's personal secretary, Dashiell Talbot, was the most trustworthy man he knew. His calm demeanor and wise counsel had been invaluable to the queen over the years. To Grantham, as well. And with his hesitations about his own courtiers still fresh in his mind…

He cleared his throat. "I do not know if anyone can help me, but I always appreciate your input. And his. So yes, we will find time when things have settled."

"There will be some normalcy after our guests depart tomorrow," his mother said.

"Almost all of them," he grunted, hating that he yet again sought Ophelia in the crowd. Now she was standing off to the side of the orchestra, surrounded by admirers, both men and women. They jostled to be near her as she smiled and held court with just as much aplomb as any queen or princess of his country had done. Maddening.

The queen followed his stare and cleared her throat. "Lady Ophelia is a pleasure. I do not regret her staying, and not just for Priscilla's sake. She brings such brightness to whatever room she enters."

He flinched at the use of the term. Yes, brightness was what she brought. Blinding at times. "Hoydens always do," he muttered, and wished he had a drink. Several drinks.

Giabella nudged him gently. "And yet you cannot take your eyes off of her. Not now and not when you were dancing earlier."

"I'm sure I don't know what you mean," he managed through clenched teeth. "Pardon me, Mama. I believe I could use some air."

He didn't wait for her response, but stepped away, hands clenching with every step he took. God's teeth, he had spent his entire life having it driven into him that a man of his position could not reveal his emotions, for good or for bad. That his mother was able to make this observation was all the more reason to simply avoid Ophelia for the remainder of her stay here.

And perhaps it was also best to avoid everyone else, too. He certainly had a great deal to do.

CHAPTER 3

"Your Majesty?"

Grantham looked up from his paperwork and found the Duke of Gilmore standing in the doorway. He stood immediately and came around the desk, hand outstretched. "Gilmore. I didn't expect to see you so early."

Gilmore shook the offered hand. "It is not so very early, Your Majesty." He motioned his head to the clock on the mantel and Grantham followed the movement. His eyes went wide as he noted the hour.

"Ah, I have lost track of the time. The guests must be readying to head to the docks. I must come join the family for all the farewells."

"Yes, a few moments more, I think. I actually slipped up here early in the hopes we might have a moment to talk alone before the departure and whatever formalities will accompany it."

Grantham nodded and motioned to the chairs before the fire. "Is something troubling you? Have Priscilla's parents been difficult?"

Both men frowned. Priscilla's parents had shown up to the island a few days before, uninvited and unwanted. They'd caused a scene and even threatened Priscilla. They'd been put in their places, of course. And it had worked itself out, after all, because it had forced Remi to admit his feelings for the woman.

Grantham would never forget the look on his often-wayward brother's face when he realized what he could lose. He had never seen such a thing. Such certainty, such deep and abiding love. And now they would marry and all signs pointed to them being very happy.

Meanwhile Gilmore had taken on the task of seeing the wretched parents back to London, with a great deal of pressure on them so that they would never cause Priscilla pain again.

"They are dreadful people," Gilmore answered. "But I can handle them. If I don't, they shall not like the way my wife does it."

"Throw them into the North Sea?" Grantham asked mildly.

"I honestly wouldn't put it past her," Gilmore laughed. "When she is protective of another person, she will do anything to see them safe. It is quite something to experience that kind of fierce loyalty."

Grantham bent his head. "I assume so. But if not our uninvited guests, what do you wish to discuss with me, Your Grace?"

Gilmore shifted. "Ophelia."

Swallowing hard, Grantham fought to keep his expression neutral. "What about her?"

"I appreciate the invitation for her to stay here a while longer," Gilmore said. "She is so close to Priscilla, I know she will love being a part of the wedding and having a little more time before they are parted for far longer than they are accustomed to experiencing. And yet...I worry about her."

"How so?"

Gilmore's brow wrinkled. "She...is very good at letting her brilliant personality shine through, but she has had a few difficult years. By herself, with her friend distracted by her own happiness, I only fear she might lose herself a little in memories."

Grantham drew back slightly. He made a study of Ophelia, almost against his own will. And he had guessed on some small level that she used her brightness to blind as much as to warm or to comfort. A rather clever instinct of self-protection, really, if opposite of his own. But now her brother was confirming this, and it made him wonder what exactly had hurt her in the past.

"What would you like me to do?" he asked since Gilmore seemed to expect a response.

"I realize you are very busy with your own work," Gilmore said with a shake of his head. "I would never expect you to trouble yourself with her, but…"

"I will make sure there is someone aware of Lady Ophelia," Grantham said softly. "Her welfare will be carefully monitored, I assure you. She will be safe and as happy as one can be during her time in Athawick without your watchful eye."

"Good." The relief on Gilmore's face was plain. "Very good." He pushed to his feet. "I should go down and say my private goodbyes to her. Abigail was doing so when I came up here and I didn't wish to interrupt."

"I will go downstairs with you," Grantham said as he motioned to the door. "I'm sure the family will gather soon for the farewells to the party at large."

They moved together, but at the door, Grantham stopped. "I did want to say to you how happy I am that you and Her Grace attended the wedding."

The duke glanced at him in what seemed like pleasure. "Thank you. It was a wonderful time."

"I do not have many…friends," Grantham continued, and hated how awkward it made him feel. "But I hope I can count you as one."

Gilmore smiled. "Indeed. You may with my great delight."

Grantham cleared his throat, seeking to be gruff once more because the more vulnerable emotion felt so odd and raw. "Off we go then."

The two men walked together, talking of nothing important as they did so. It was somewhat frustrating to Grantham. He couldn't pry. Not to Ophelia's brother, not without being far too obvious in his attraction to her. But he wanted to know what had inspired such concern for her. What had happened in her life that made Gilmore worry so about her?

And how could Grantham find out?

They reached the bottom of the stairs and, indeed, the family was already gathered. He shook Gilmore's hand again and stepped into the line, watching as Gilmore moved into a parlor.

"Lady Ophelia is already in there with the Duchess of Gilmore," his mother explained in a whisper. "They are such a close family, it's lovely to see, but I think Lady Ophelia is suffering a little to think of being parted from them for a few weeks."

Grantham grunted his response but leaned forward slightly. From this angle he could see just into the parlor and caught a glimpse of a woman's skirt. Ophelia's or the duchess's, he could not say. He leaned a little more but there was nothing else within his sightline.

At last, the Gilmore party stepped into the hall, and Grantham noted that the duke and duchess both had red eyes, as if the farewell had been emotional. Ophelia followed them, and when they stepped aside he finally got a good look at her. She, too, was wiping away tears. Seeing them he felt a swell of desire to…comfort her somehow. Such an odd feeling for someone who could be so entirely frustrating.

She smiled at her brother and sister-in-law one more time, and then her gaze flitted to him. He held there a beat, until she blushed and then rushed from the hallway. Gilmore sighed as he stepped up the line, saying farewell to the rest of the family. When he and the duchess reached Grantham, he bowed and she curtseyed.

"It has been wonderful," the duchess said with a genuine smile for him and for his mother. "I hope it is an experience we get to repeat many times."

She slipped to the door, and Gilmore hesitated. "Thank you again."

Grantham inclined his head. "And I will most definitely take care of what we spoke of earlier. Do not worry. Safe travels."

They exited and the queen leaned up to him, her voice low as the rest of the visiting parties began to filter through the line. "What did you two speak of?"

He shifted. He could easily tell his mother what Gilmore asked regarding Ophelia. She would take responsibility for her—the queen made no secret that she liked Ophelia. And yet he didn't tell her. Instead he shrugged. "Oh, just something about shipping. Nothing to worry about."

She accepted the lie and focused her attention on the guests who were beginning to reach the head of the line. Grantham said his goodbyes, too, but it was all rote. His mind moved from the task at hand, taking itself elsewhere. To places it ought not go.

To thoughts of Ophelia, and how much he wanted to know some of the secrets she hid beneath her wide smile and maddening eyes.

Despite the emotionality of the morning's departures, Ophelia couldn't help but smile as she watched Priscilla practically bounce in pure excitement as a beleaguered seamstress pinched and pinned fabric around her trembling body. Her friend was being fitted for her wedding gown, and already the dress was impossibly beautiful.

"You're a vision, dearest," Ophelia said.

Priscilla looked over and at her. "I hope so. I want how happy I am to be reflected in my face, in my gown, in everything about me."

Ophelia's smile broadened. "And it is. Goodness, I've known you almost all my life and I've seen you through trying times. I've never seen you so content. More than content. Your joy is palpable and I am so happy for you. You deserve nothing but the best."

"As do you," Priscilla said. "Now that I've had this remarkable feeling, my only hope is that you will be able to experience the same someday soon."

Ophelia pursed her lips. "Well, I don't know about that. I have not met my prince yet, I don't think."

She said the words, but her mind conjured up an image of Grantham as she spoke. Staring down at her intently. Making everything in the world but him fade into the background.

She blinked the thought away as Priscilla said, "Well, who is to say? You had quite a crowd of admirers last night. Including the king."

"Oh yes, the king." Ophelia rolled her eyes. "He is no admirer of mine and you know it."

"You were dancing with him," Priscilla insisted, catching her gaze. "And you two looked quite intent."

"Well, he asked me for some unknown reason," Ophelia huffed. "I could not think of a reason to refuse." As she spoke, she could almost feel his fingers trace along her hip, his body brush hers as they moved together.

"Are you well?" Priscilla asked, her expression growing concerned.

Ophelia shrugged. "Of course, why would I not be?"

"You gasped," Priscilla said. "Just now."

"Oh." Ophelia hadn't realized she had done that. "It was nothing, I assure you. Just as the dance was nothing. I have no idea what I did to inspire his regard. He is never anything but unpleasant."

The seamstress made a soft noise in her throat and Ophelia caught herself. Gracious, she was being rude and she hadn't truly meant to be. But this woman was Grantham's subject and his servant. And from everything Ophelia had observed since her arrival in Athawick, those who worked for the king seemed intensely loyal to him.

One tiny mark in his favor, she supposed, though she gave it reluctantly.

"I am impressed, Miss Steele," Ophelia said, trying to make up for what she'd said. "You have done magnificent work in a short amount of time. The royal family must keep you on your toes with last minute demands."

The seamstress smiled over at her, though her gaze remained somewhat wary. "Thank you, my lady. And I'm nothing but pleased to serve the royal family, I assure you. There will be no finer king than our current one, not for a hundred years or more, I think."

Ophelia nodded. She had been put in her place and she probably deserved it. If she wished to complain about Grantham she would do better to do it alone with Priscilla. Not that she got to be alone with her much anymore. Though they still technically shared a room, it was no secret that Priscilla spent her nights in Remi's chambers.

"The king is well loved by his subjects," Priscilla said.

Miss Steele wrinkled her brow. "On the whole, yes."

There was a hesitation to those words that caught Ophelia's attention. There had been murmurs about some unrest in the country since her arrival. She'd heard Nathan and Abigail whispering about it, as well.

Miss Steele made a mark on the fabric and stepped back to look Priscilla up and down. "I think it needs more of the lace. Let me fetch some and I'll be back."

She stepped from the room and Priscilla tilted her head at Ophelia. "Dearest, you mustn't be so bold in your opinions about Grantham. This is not our country."

"Yes, I know," Ophelia sighed. "It was badly done of me. He is just the most frustrating—" She cut herself off because Priscilla's brows had both lifted. "But Miss Steele did let a little information slip. I've heard talk about some trouble in the kingdom. Do you know more about it now that you spend your nights in the prince's bed?"

Priscilla's eyes went wide. "Ophelia!"

"Why do you look shocked? You're the one doing it," Ophelia said with a laugh. "And good for you. You are happy and there is nothing in the world I want more for you."

Priscilla's expression softened, though her cheeks were still pink with the subject. "I *am* happy. Deliriously happy. As to your question…all I know is that the king is troubled. But he will not talk to anyone about it."

"That seems right," Ophelia said with a roll of her eyes. "So pompous that he thinks he's the only one who could possibly have an answer."

"You so quickly dismiss him," Priscilla said gently. "And yet you cannot stop watching him."

For a moment there was only silence in the room as Ophelia stared at her friend. Finally she drew a deep breath. "That…that is not true."

"Isn't it?" Priscilla asked, and she arched a brow.

Ophelia shifted. Normally she was the observant one, the one offering unsolicited advice and gentle judgment. To have the same turned on her was rather uncomfortable, truth be told.

Luckily she didn't have to answer the charge, because Miss Steele re-entered the chamber and the focus returned to Priscilla's gown. And yet even as Ophelia cooed and smiled over how utterly gorgeous Priscilla was in both her gown and her joy, she couldn't help but think about Grantham, just as she had been charged with doing.

The only time she'd felt any power over the odd sensations that crowded her chest when she was near him was when she had toyed with him at the ball. Flummoxing him kept him from coming too near. He hated that about her, after all. So perhaps it would be best to keep doing just that during her remaining time in Athawick.

That and avoiding him entirely. Even though this was his country, his palace, his kingdom.

CHAPTER 4

As soon as Priscilla had finished with her fitting, she flitted off to meet with Remi. Oh, her friend claimed they were going over wedding arrangements, but the brightness of her eyes had made Ophelia believe that they were doing something far more pleasurable and wicked with their afternoon.

A twinge of jealousy worked through her as she stepped out into the garden and drew a long breath of cool late summer air. Pleasure was not something she'd had a great deal of experience with, at least not physically. She knew what it felt like, of course. She had touched herself in the night, twisting in her sheets as she reached for that little blinding explosion deep inside of her.

But when it came to men...well, that was more complicated. A lady, at least a lady in England, was meant to be chaste. That was currency in her country. If one squandered it...

She shivered and pushed those thoughts away. They were meaningless, after all. Pleasure was not the in cards for her at present. Certainly not the kind that went along with love, like Priscilla had found. Ophelia had put her hopes for that kind of future away four long years before.

She strolled through the garden, trying to shift her focus onto the beauty around her. Normally that wasn't such a difficult task. She liked to lose herself in her surroundings, let her mind go wild with ideas and hopes and dreams.

But today it kept going back to one place, one person. She huffed out a breath as she rounded a corner and came to a complete stop. A sculpture had been placed in the midst of a round of low bushes before her.

"Of course," she muttered as she moved toward it and looked, reading the plaque aloud so she could hear it. "King Grantham, eighth of his line."

She let her gaze slide up the stone figure, clad in what seemed to be traditional robes from generations ago. The body was not as big as the real thing, nor as toned. She could tell that even through the folds of stone fabric. Odd, really, since most of the time these sorts of statues were meant to idealize their subject rather than reflect or diminish him.

He had one hand on his hip, the other was extended, a finger pointing to some unknown horizon.

But the face...

She stepped close and lifted up on her tiptoes. The face was very good. It looked so much like him that she drank in the details that she normally kept herself from staring at when the real man stood before her. The angled jawline feathered here with an expertly sculpted beard. The full lips that seemed so perfect for kissing. The sharp gaze, only slightly muted by stone. She sucked in a breath and moved closer, resting a hand on the outstretched stone finger to balance herself as she leaned in.

Only to have the entire finger suddenly snap off in her hand, sending her stumbling away from the statue.

She froze, staring down at the detached digit, angled accusingly toward her, as if to proclaim that she was the culprit.

"Merde," she muttered beneath her breath as her thumb brushed the rough stone. "Damn!"

She stepped up to the statue again and tried to press the broken piece of stone against the ragged edge left behind. Of course it would not reattach, not by the miracle of hope, at any rate.

She pondered her options. She could just…pocket the finger. Hope no one would notice. Or drop it on the grass, leaving it unclear who might have damaged it. Of course that might lead to trouble for some poor gardener. She didn't think the royal family would be too harsh on someone, but who knew? And what if someone had seen her here, from the window or some other place in the garden?

She tried to push the finger back in place yet again when Grantham himself rushed past the little statuary, hands clenched at his sides, face stormy with emotion.

She squeaked in terror and shoved the broken piece of finger behind her back as he stopped dead in his tracks and pivoted back toward her. The storm in his gaze faded, but only a fraction, as he stared her up and down, then glanced over to his statue.

God's teeth, did he notice the broken piece? She was about to find out because he moved her way in a few long steps and came to halt before her.

"Lady Ophelia," Grantham said, smoothing his jacket as he came to a stop before her. "Good afternoon."

She inclined her head. "Good afternoon, Your Majesty."

He hesitated, trying to find something to say. He'd been trying to escape news of unrest when he saw her standing in front of his statue in the garden. It had been quite the surprise, enough to draw him to her. And yet he had planned nothing for this encounter after that.

"Wonderful…er…weather we are having today," she said.

He wrinkled his brow. She was shifting slightly, hands clasped behind her back as she looked anywhere but him. And though they always had a tension between them, this felt different somehow.

"Indeed," he managed. "An Athawickian late summer is my favorite season, I admit. The air is still warm, but one may feel the bite of coolness in the breeze. The leaves are threatening to turn. It's a season of possibility."

Her eyes went wide and her attention shifted back to his face. "I think that may be the most words you have ever strung together when speaking to me."

He blinked at the directness of her statement. Not that he expected anything less from her. Over the months they'd known each other she had often treated him not as a king, but as an adversary she sparred with.

"That...that is likely true. Unlike my brother, I am not unnecessarily verbose."

She nodded slowly. "That seems reasonable, considering your position. If you had a long, drawn out conversation with everyone who crossed your path, you would get nothing done at all." She shuffled slightly. She had not removed her hands from behind her back yet. "And I would not keep you now, sir."

"You want me to go away," Grantham said slowly, suspicion growing inside of him. Why was she being so odd? "Why?"

"Of course I don't," she protested, sputtering as if he had made far worse an accusation against her character. "Gracious, I care little for what you do. Go, stay, it is your palace. Your...your garden."

"My statue?" he pressed, and watched pink enter her cheeks. A very fetching color, indeed.

"Is it?" she asked. "I hadn't noticed."

"Hadn't you?" he pressed, starting to enjoy himself a little. He rarely...played anymore. He didn't tease, not even his siblings. He hadn't for years. His father had wrung all that out of him, replacing it with cruel expectations of comportment and visions of perfection that could never be attained - no matter how he tried - then or now.

But this woman brought something out in him. Made him forget himself.

"Not at all," she insisted. "I was only walking through the

garden." She cast a very quick look at the statue over her shoulder. Not long enough to really see it. "And so it is you. How lovely. Thank you for pointing it out. Your palace really is a wonder."

He arched a brow but did not respond. Ophelia didn't like silence, he knew. So if he speared her with it, she might let him know why in the world she was being so strange.

She pursed her lips. "I think I shall continue my stroll in the garden, and I do not wish to keep you from what I am certain is very important business. Kingly duty." She was nodding now, her shifting increasing. "I'm certain I could never understand in the slightest."

"Ophelia," he said softly.

She froze and stared up at him. He realized that was the first time he had ever called her by her name without the honorific before it. Entirely inappropriate. And yet he did love the way her name tasted on his tongue.

She cleared her throat and huffed out a breath. "Fine, I cannot hide it any longer. You have caught me."

"Caught you?" he repeated, confusion and interest mounting in equal measure. "What do you mean?"

The pink of her cheeks was darkening to red as she drew her hands from behind her back. One fist was clenched, and she turned it over and opened her fingers, revealing…

"Is that my finger?" he asked, staring at the marble digit she'd been gripping so tightly that it had left an indentation in her palm.

"Yes," she grumbled. "Well, the statue's finger, at any rate."

He stared at it a moment more and then tilted his head back and laughed. He laughed harder than he had in years and it was like a world of worry and guilt rolled off of him in that moment. She didn't join him, simply stared at him as he fought to regain control over his faculties.

"You have a very nice laugh, Your Majesty," she said softly, when he had gotten himself back together.

"Thank you," he said, shifting with slight discomfort that she had seen him in that state. "But do not think you can distract me from my interrogation with compliments, my lady."

She arched a brow and a flutter of a smile tilted the corner of her lips. "Interrogation. Is that what this is?"

"There has been a crime, has there not?" he pressed. "Assault against the image of a king."

He had not given his tone a playful edge in so long he feared he might not know how to do it anymore, but she seemed to understand because now she did flash one of those bright, glorious smiles, if only briefly.

"A serious charge, yes," she agreed solemnly. "I wish you luck in finding the culprit."

"Do you deny it was you?" he asked. "Despite holding the evidence in your very hand?"

She shrugged. "I suppose that *is* damning, yes."

He realized he'd moved a little closer to her as they spoke. Not too close yet, but heading that way. He stopped himself and for a moment they merely stared at each other. Good God, but she was beautiful. It almost hurt to look at her.

He cleared his throat. "Do you want to tell me how you came to be holding the finger from my statue?"

"No, I do not," she said softly. "But since I'm certain you can have me cast out to sea or put on a rack for withholding the information, I *will* tell you. I was…examining the statue and I reached up to balance myself on the finger and it…broke…off."

"How close were you to the statue that you had to balance yourself?" he asked, imagining her perched up close to his face. His real face, not the stone one behind her.

She pursed her lips, drawing his attention to them. "Close enough."

"I see."

There was another long silence, and she shook her head. "H-here, let me give you this," she stammered.

He stepped toward her at the exact moment she moved in his

direction, and they nearly collided in the middle. She brought herself up short and stared up at him, as close as she had been when he was dancing with her the previous night. Only right now they were alone and the distance would not be considered appropriate by chaperones. Not that there were any of those around.

She swallowed, her bright blue eyes so like the sea as she stared up at him that he lost his breath. Her hand trembled as she held out the broken piece of the statue, pressing it into his palm. He had foregone gloves for his walk. She also was not wearing any, so her skin brushed across his, warm and soft, far too intimate a gesture. The touch sent electric awareness up his arm, pleasure that settled in the most inopportune places.

"G-good afternoon, Your Majesty," she whispered.

"Good afternoon, my lady," he said, watching as she pivoted and hustled away toward the house.

He stared at the broken statue piece in his hand and then carefully placed it in his jacket pocket where the weight of it served as a reminder of this encounter.

He drew in a deep breath and started back along his path through the garden. But he no longer felt frustrated by encounters with courtiers or decisions that had to be made in the government. For the first time in a very long time, he felt...*free.*

CHAPTER 5

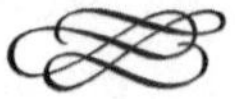

Ophelia stood beside the mantel in the parlor, outside the circle of the royal family. They had shared a meal that night and she had been transfixed by their transformation. From formal hosts, they had become a family, laughing and joking with each other. Even Queen Giabella's longtime secretary had joined them, and Ophelia could see how much he was loved and accepted as a member of their circle. She would have counted it as a fine time, except...

Well, except for Grantham. He had been quiet during the meal, not participating in the fun around him. And he'd gone back to his old habits: watching her, his expression frustratingly unreadable. Did he like her? Hate her? Want to kiss her?

"Oh, why do you have to bring that into it?" she chided herself softly, careful not to look at him across the room. She'd been doing far too much of that.

Priscilla caught her eye and smiled before she stepped away from the group and went to Ophelia, sliding an arm through hers. "How are you?"

Ophelia blinked. "Very well, thank you."

"Are you certain? You have been a little...odd today," Priscilla pressed. "I cannot tell if it is a bit of melancholy at the departure of Gilmore and Abigail or…or something else."

She now glanced pointedly toward Grantham, and Ophelia huffed out a breath. The last thing she needed was Priscilla putting her nose in this. If she did, there was no doubt Prince Remington would follow, and Grantham would hate that. Ophelia would certainly be to blame for it in his mind.

"I'm perfectly well," she insisted. "My oddness is all in your head."

She said the words strenuously enough, but they were a lie. Of course she had been odd. She had been entirely thrown off guard by her encounter with Grantham in the garden. By that flutter she'd felt low in her belly when he laughed. She knew what the flutter was. And if she were honest with herself, it wasn't the first time she'd felt it in the king's company, either.

"I believe your soon-to-be husband is trying to call you to his side," she said, motioning toward the settee where Remi was staring intently at Priscilla.

Her friend blushed, ducking her head. "I assume at some point he will be less obvious in his ardor."

"I doubt it," Ophelia said, turning her toward him. "Now go sit with him, chat with your future family. I am going to take a breath of air. Clear my head so I won't be, as you put it, *odd*."

She could see Priscilla wished to say more, but she laughed when Ophelia gave her a gentle shove away and didn't resist, making her way to take her place beside Remi. Their hands tangled together before he lifted her knuckles to his lips for a brief kiss.

Ophelia turned away from the casual intimacy with a blush. Great God, she needed to get her mind back in order. She slipped across the room to the double doors leading to the terrace. She stepped outside and shut them softly behind her, praying everyone had been so tangled up in their conversation that they hadn't noticed her departure. She hadn't dared to look at Grantham to see if he had still been watching her. Staring her down, more like it.

The terrace on the back side of the estate was remarkable. It covered the entire length of the palace, so one could step out from a great many rooms for air, walk the entire length of marble and even slip down to the garden. Not that she wanted to go to the garden any time soon.

Now it had memories and she was trying to pretend that wasn't true.

She huffed out a breath and began to make her way from the parlor toward a more darkened corner of the parapet. She had only taken a few steps when the parlor door opened. She glanced back to see Grantham had exited behind her.

"Blast the man," she muttered, and hurried toward the shadows more quickly. Perhaps his exit was not related to hers. Yes, that could be possible. And if he didn't see her, she could escape here for a moment and not face—

"Lady Ophelia?" he called out.

She froze and turned back. She was half in the shadows now, but they offered her no protection. He was staring at her openly.

"What is it?" she snapped, harsher than she'd meant to sound.

"What are you doing?" he asked.

She folded her arms. "I am trying to escape you, if you must know. It is unconscionable that you are refusing to allow it."

He froze, his expression becoming wild for the briefest of moments before he corrected it back to his usual impassive one. "I apologize sincerely. I will go back inside the house."

He was truly upset by the idea that he had done something untoward by following her. A unique reaction. How many men had simply stalked her across ballrooms or gardens even when she told them she wished to be alone?

She moved toward him. "Wait. You are here, Your Majesty, and you do not deserve my ire. I apologize. Of course you needn't go back inside."

He hesitated. "I was not trying to violate your privacy, but I did wish to discuss something with you, if you would allow it." He cleared his throat. "Confess something."

She caught her breath. *Confess.* That was a uniquely loaded word, wasn't it? A person could confess a wrong or a secret…or a desire. And that he wished to direct this apparent confession toward her was intriguing.

She nodded. "If you would like."

He motioned her to continue the way she had begun, away from the parlor, into the soft darkness on the outer edge of the terrace. He followed at a respectful distance, and when she stepped up to the stone railing and rested her hands there, he moved beside her and placed his own just a fraction down the way. She felt the warmth of them, even though that could not be actually possible.

"What is your confession?" she asked, breathless now.

He glanced toward her, then pivoted to face her. They were closer now, his body almost brushing hers. She could feel the faint warmth of his breath against her cheek as he whispered, "The statue in the garden is a strange thing."

She wrinkled her brow. "I…don't think so. There are statues of kings all over London."

"Yes, but the one in the garden has been standing there for at least two hundred years," he insisted.

She shook her head. "How would someone know two hundred years ago that *you* would be king someday?"

"They carved the statue for King Bartholomew, the first king to reside in this palace," he explained. "Horrible man. One of the worst. I can direct you to a book if you'd like to know more about him, but it is not nighttime reading. It will give you nightmares."

She blinked. He was certainly verbose all of a sudden. And she… liked it. She liked the warm tenor of his voice and the way he held her gaze as he spoke to her.

"And his son," he continued, "who eventually became King David, despised him. When the father died, the son had his statue's head…removed, and replaced with his own head."

Her eyes went wide. "What?"

"Yes. I suppose that petty action would have been the end of it, but David was killed during a naval battle he insisted on being part of. His death marked the end of a war and his brother, King Samuel, took over. There was to be a soiree and the head was hurriedly replaced with that of the new king. And hence, a tradition was born, and a dozen kings afterward would do the same. So you see, my lady, the finger you detached this afternoon in the garden…was not mine."

"I see," she breathed. "Well, *that* changes everything." Another of those near-smiles tilted the corner of his lips and she felt herself wanting to lean closer. She fought the urge. "Was *that* what you wished to confess, sir?"

"No," he said slowly. "Well…yes and no. You see, when I was fifteen and Remi twelve, we were roughhousing in the garden near what was then my father's statue and, well…" He cleared his throat. "*I* broke that very same finger off."

Her mouth dropped open, for she could see what was coming next.

"My father was not exactly an understanding sort, and he would have been enraged that I was behaving so poorly. Remi had the brilliant idea to use paste to repair it. And it has stayed fixed, somehow, through wind, rain and snow for fifteen long years. Until you, Lady Ophelia, created a storm that could not be resisted." He inclined his head. "But you did not break the statue. I did. And I could not allow you to believe otherwise."

She covered her mouth with one hand, but she could not contain the giggles that escaped around her fingers. They gave way to a belly laugh at the very idea of it all. She glanced up to see if he was also laughing, but he wasn't. No, he was just standing there, watching her as always…only this time his expression was anything but unreadable.

His pupils were dilated, his expression lined with desire. Oh yes, that was desire, unmistakable and undeniable. She felt it too. Down to her bones, through every part of her body. And when he edged a tiny bit closer, when he lifted an ungloved hand to trace the line of her jaw, she couldn't stop herself from shivering with pleasure.

He bent his head slowly, his fingers cupping her chin to tilt her toward him. She didn't resist. If anything, she lifted on her tiptoes, trying to reach him faster. Needing to find his mouth with a desperation that shook her to her very core.

Their lips met and the world ceased to exist. It was only his mouth on hers, gentle for the briefest of moment, then more insistent as he placed a hand on her hip and drew her even closer. She wound her arms around his neck, lifting into his broad chest and parting her lips beneath his.

He made a rumbling sound deep down, one that called to her own sigh of pleasure and then he wasn't gentle anymore. His tongue drove forward, plundering with a desperation that she matched. He tilted his head, probing deeper, tasting her, savoring her, and she was utterly lost.

That thought jolted her. She had been utterly lost before, after all. To her great detriment. She broke their mouths and staggered back, staring up at him as she clenched her shaking hands at her sides.

"I—" she began but could think of no words. So instead, she pivoted on her heel and raced away.

Grantham watched as Ophelia raced past the parlor door that would take her back to the family and disappeared into the darkness on the other side of the terrace.

"Fuck," he muttered, spinning back to the low stone wall where he gripped his fists against the rough surface. His lips felt like they were on fire. Hell, his entire body was on fire, burning for this woman who confounded him regularly.

"Your Majesty?"

He jumped at the sound of Blairford's voice behind him, and drew a long breath before he turned to face the courtier. If Blairford had seen anything between Grantham and Ophelia, his expression did not reveal it. Of course, his expression never did. Something that had become more troublesome with each passing day.

"What is it, Blairford?" Grantham asked quietly.

"I have an update about the separatist group, and you said you wished me to come to you as soon as I had it."

Grantham shook off his response to Ophelia as best he could and nodded. "I asked you to find me a leader I could meet with, to address the concerns of those who wish me not to be king. Does this mean you have found someone?"

The flicker across the other man's face answered the question far before his words did. "Er...no, Your Majesty," Blairford admitted. "It is not that simple."

"Isn't it?" Grantham asked. "It seems markedly simple to me. We are not an enormous country, Blairford. A few days' ride from one end the other. In most of the areas of the island, everyone knows everyone else. If you cannot manage this, perhaps it is time I find someone who can."

At that Blairford's expression darkened, and Grantham recognized a flare of...hate in his eyes. This man hated him, at least in the moment. Which did nothing to increase his trust of the courtier.

"That is unnecessary, Your Majesty," Blairford said, and the expression was gone now, not a remnant left behind. "I only wish your permission to use more...strenuous methods of uncovering the identity of whoever is in charge."

Grantham pursed his lips. "You mean violent means. You wish to threaten in my name. That is intolerable. Find another way."

Blairford inclined his head and began to walk away, but he'd only gotten a few steps when he stopped and turned back. "May I speak plainly, Your Majesty?"

Grantham arched a brow. "Please."

"If you could save a thousand of your people by sacrificing one, would you do it?"

Grantham wrinkled his brow. "Not without exhausting every other method at my disposal. You see, that is the difference between you and me, and those who would encourage me to use my power as a club. I refuse to devalue one for many. Not until there is no other choice."

Blairford pinched his lips and nodded slowly. "Then it remains to be seen how history will judge that decision, sir. Good evening."

Grantham watched him go, his chest burning with frustration for everything that had happened tonight. He'd always valued loyalty…trust. And now he wasn't certain where to properly place any of it.

"Perhaps the real person you cannot trust is yourself," he muttered as he began to make his way across the terrace, himself. Only he didn't stop at the parlor, where he could see his family still gathered. Sasha had gone to the piano and was playing a jig as the others danced together and laughed.

No, he couldn't go back into that room because they would see how torn he was about their country, how torn he was about Ophelia. He couldn't let them see. Instead, he went to the terrace door that led to his study. He would work tonight and fulfill his duties first, as he had been taught to do.

He would work tonight, and somehow that would make him forget.

CHAPTER 6

Ophelia had hoped that if she read a book and had a good night's sleep and pretended she'd never kissed the King of Athawick, the memories would fade into the back of her mind.

A failure if ever she had experienced one.

It wasn't that she hadn't tried. She had returned to her chamber and sent a quick note to the family that she was tired and wouldn't return to their fun. She had picked up the book she'd been reading during her stay and stared at the same sentence fifteen times before she tossed it aside in frustration.

And when she readied for bed and blew out her candle? She hadn't slept. No, she'd just relived Grantham leaning in toward her. The pressure of his lips against hers. The taste of him that lingered on her tongue.

And now as she paced the breakfast room the next morning, she still thought of the same thing. Her mind raced with questions:

Why had he kissed her?

Why had she kissed him back?

What would happen now?

What did it all mean?

"Good morning, Lady Ophelia."

She jumped as Remi entered the room, a broad smile on his face. "Remi…Prince Remington, Your Highness," she stammered.

He stopped and stared at her. "Remi is fine, Ophelia. After all, you and my soon-to-be wife are as close as sisters. We will be family in a matter of days."

"Yes," she said, glad to grasp on to this far more pleasant topic. "I cannot wait."

He motioned to the sideboard where a selection of breakfast delicacies had been placed. Ophelia had been in the room five minutes and not even looked at them.

"God's teeth, they do make a spread," Remi murmured. "I am rarely up early enough to be here for it."

Ophelia smiled as she looked over the food before her. She was still so anxious she could scarcely think of eating. "If you are not normally an early riser, what brings you up today?"

He gave her a half-smile and put a few of what Ophelia recognized as Priscilla's favorites on his plate. "I think you can guess."

She felt her cheeks heat slightly, but she laughed. "Well, you two are not very good at keeping secrets. She has not slept in our shared chamber since your marriage was announced. But why did she send you to fetch her breakfast? I'm sure you could have asked a servant."

"The lady very sweetly believes that no one will be the wiser if *I* fetch a plate for us to share," he said. "And I could never disabuse her of such a notion."

Ophelia tilted her head. "You truly do love her."

"I do." His tone became serious. "With all that I am."

Ophelia pondered him a moment, her mind taking her back to a man she had once believed could love her so completely but hadn't. And to Grantham, who might kiss her on terraces but would surely never allow his heart to thaw enough to want more than that.

Not that she wanted more than that from him. She didn't even understand why he'd kissed her. Was it part of some ruse or game to him? That thought annoyed her to no end.

"Your expression has become very taut," Remi said with a half-laugh. "Do you disapprove the match?"

"Gracious, no," Ophelia said. "Priscilla is happy and I think you will make it your life's pursuit to keep her that way. I could ask for nothing more for her."

He nodded. "May I ask what is troubling you then?"

Ophelia hesitated. This man was too observant to be put off with some empty platitude. "Just a question about your brother, I suppose."

"My brother?" Remi repeated. "Did our esteemed monarch offend you in some way last night?"

Her eyes went wide. "Why…why would you ask me that?"

His brow wrinkled. "Because you each went onto the terrace at the same time and then you went to your chamber and he to his study to work. Since everyone knows you two are somewhat at odds, there was some question amongst the family as if you had an unpleasant encounter."

"Not unpleasant," Ophelia murmured, and tried not to relive that kiss yet again. This was really getting ridiculous. "But I do need to speak to the king, I realize. Do you know where he is?"

Remi's expression faltered a little. "Back in his study, one must assume. He does not exactly keep me in the know when it comes to his schedule, I fear. He doesn't seem to believe any of his family could be of assistance in his problems." He looked off in the distance a moment. "I do worry about him."

Ophelia's ire faded a fraction at that very real expression of concern. Remi was so rarely serious that one had to pay attention when he was. He was truly worried about his brother. And she herself began to wonder at Grantham's state of mind.

She cleared her throat. "If I have never seen you before at breakfast, I've also never seen him. Does he also lay about in bed?"

Remi snorted out a laugh. "Indeed not. He's in his study from the break of dawn, if not earlier." He lifted his plate. "Normally I would escort you there, but my lady awaits."

"You must not disappoint her," Ophelia said with a smile. "Tell her that your secret is safe with me."

He gave a half-salute and headed out the door, plate in hand, bounce in his step. But the moment he was gone, her smile fell and she glanced from the room. Just down the hall was Grantham's study. How she knew its exact location from almost any room in the palace was not a fact she wished to dissect at present.

What she did need to do was speak to the man. Directly address what had occurred between them and figure out what to do about it. She drew a deep breath and stepped from the room. Her hands shook as she made her way up the hallway until she reached the ornate door that led to the king's study.

With a deep breath, she knocked. There was no answer immediately, so she worried her lip. He might not even be in there and then she would have to set out to look for him. With a frown, she tapped the door open just to verify.

He was seated at a huge cherrywood desk, bent over paperwork, so focused that she doubted he'd even heard her knock. He looked… sick. He looked worn down. In that moment she had never seen him so troubled and all her emotion softened toward him. She wanted to help somehow, though she had no idea how a person in her position could ever do that. He kept such a distance from her at all times.

Well, except when he kissed her. But that was once. He had never expressed any interest before that. So why would he accept her assistance now?

"What are you doing here?" he snapped, and his gaze lifted to snare hers.

She jolted at the sharp tone of his voice and the fire in his eyes, but somehow found the strength to step into the room rather than go racing away from him as she had done the night before.

"I'm sorry to intrude," she said as she pushed the door partly shut behind her, trying to find privacy but not impropriety. It felt a precarious balance with this man. "I-I simply wished to speak to you and was told you might be in your study this morning."

"Working," he said softly. "You know you can make an appointment with my courtiers if you need to speak to me. Or better yet, discuss any complaints you have with my staff."

She wrinkled her brow. Twelve hours ago he had been ravaging her mouth with his tongue, and now he spoke to her like she was a recalcitrant houseguest. And perhaps she was, at that, but still. It was very rude of him.

She folded her arms. "You wish me to speak to your staff about the kiss?"

His eyebrows shot up and he lunged to his feet, stalking around the desk and past her to slam the door fully. Now he was rising over her, uncommonly handsome and outrageously tall and broad. The man filled every room he came into with his form and his presence, and now he appeared to be lording it over her. She could scarcely breathe, but it wasn't from fear.

She almost wished it were.

"Have a care, my lady," he hissed. "I do not think either of us wants the news of our…our encounter to be spread throughout the household."

She stared up at him, holding his gaze as he had done to her so many times in the months they'd known each other. Today he was the one who looked away first. "What is wrong with you, Grantham?"

He flinched. "You are speaking to a king."

She shook her head. "I do not think I am. Right now I'm speaking to the man who kissed me. The *man* whose tension I can feel physically. *What* is wrong?"

He hesitated, and for a brief, wild moment she thought he might tell her. That he might collapse all those barriers he kept so high around himself and give over some hidden part of himself to her.

Then he stepped away and the spell was broken. He moved back to his desk and retook his seat. "Nothing," he said softly. "Except that I have been interrupted in my very important duties."

She pursed her lips. She was being dismissed by him…as always. And it stung far deeper after that kiss.

"I will be brief then. Why did you kiss me…Your Majesty?"

He flinched again, like he didn't like her use of his title any more than the lack of it earlier. "Ophelia," he said, his tone a low and rough warning.

"Why?" she repeated.

He looked up at her, and again she saw the cracks in him. The broken little places where she could still glimpse a man behind the crown. But he covered him. Froze him out. One day she feared he would erase him completely and be hardly more than the stone statue in the garden.

"I have no idea, my lady," he said coolly. His gaze flickered over her face, unreadable as always. "A moment's weakness, I suppose. Will that be all?"

She sucked in a breath at his utter disregard for her and what had happened between them. It…it…hurt her feelings because she wanted him to feel something about that kiss, as she did. But no. She wouldn't be so foolish. She tamped the hurt down, seeking some other emotion to cover it.

Anger. Yes, that would do. She was annoyed by him, irritated by him, frustrated by him…but not hurt. *Never* hurt. She'd let one man do that in her past, she wouldn't repeat the past with this one. This pompous arse who needed to be brought down a peg.

And she knew how to do it, didn't she? Knew all the ways she annoyed him. Why not play into them instead of avoid them? Show him that his disregard meant as little to her as their kiss did to him? She'd rather be at war with him than whatever cocktail of emotion swirled in her heart at present.

"That will be all, *Your Majesty*," she said, and executed a curtsey so low that her knees nearly touched the ground. He watched, eyes widening, filled with confusion and a touch of concern as she pivoted and left the room, closing the door none-too-gently behind her.

Good, let him be concerned. Because she had a few weeks left on this island…and she was certainly going to use them to her best advantage before she went away and never saw his rude, arrogant, *beautiful* face again.

~

Drinking at nine in the morning was never a good sign. Grantham knew it, but he still held a glass of sherry in his hand, swirling the amber liquid as he stared out the window. He had dozens of duties to attend to. There was a meeting with representatives for the sailors to prepare for, a speech to write for a few weeks from now when he awarded a medal to a member of the navy, and the pile of correspondence on his desk was legion. Despite all that, here he was, watching Ophelia as she trounced across the lawn, her upset clear in every line of her body.

Her absolutely tempting body. She had left him a quarter of an hour before, angry enough to spit, and all he wanted to do was go after her. All he wanted to do was take back that claim that the kiss meant nothing. To tell her exactly what was going on in his life and his kingdom, to tell her that he wanted her to distract him with more of those kisses.

To drown in her and never resurface for air.

His grip tightened on the glass and he pivoted away from the window, slamming it down on his desk hard enough that liquid sloshed onto the wooden surface.

"Good God, you are in a state."

He glanced up and pursed his lips as Jonah Crawford, Ilaria's husband and the new Count of the Southern Realm of Athawick, stepped into his study and shut the door behind him.

"Does no one make appointments anymore?" Grantham grumbled.

Jonah's eyebrows both lifted. "Are you angry because you're

consuming alcohol at an indecent hour or consuming alcohol because you're angry?"

"Pick one," Grantham said, slowly and succinctly. "What do you want, Jonah?"

"To help." Jonah took a seat across from him without asking his leave and Grantham rubbed his fingers at his temples. This family would kill him. And then Lady Ophelia would pick his bones clean. It was a conspiracy, surely.

"Help with what?" he asked. "I don't need any help."

"Bollocks." Jonah leaned back. "Now listen, I realize you want to keep your troubles from the family, that you think you have to bear all the weight of this uprising on your own. But you don't. It has come to affect us all. My wife was nearly killed, as was Sasha. So we all have a vested interest. And considering I am now count of the very region where I have heard the trouble originates from, it seems it is my duty in that role to help, as well. So talk."

Grantham stared at him a beat. Two. "You are...not incorrect that you should have information. The title of count is mostly ceremonial, but not entirely. And if you and Ilaria are going to make a tour of the part of this country that you now...er...lead, then I suppose a report on the issues there must be made." He sighed. "Normally I would ask Blairford to compile one, but..."

Jonah arched a brow as he trailed off. "But you don't trust him."

"How do you know that?" Grantham asked.

"I am no fool, for one. And for the other, Remi told Ilaria about what happened a few days ago. When Priscilla was attacked by her parents, endangered by her father...Blairford admitted to telling them where she was, didn't he?"

Grantham pursed his lips. "Yes. He did. He claimed it was a misunderstanding on his part."

Jonah shook his head. "It doesn't feel like one."

Grantham thought of his head courtier. Blairford was a tall, thin man with a plethora of experience in his duties. He had served under the previous king. He knew all the secrets, all the lies. He had power and he liked it. Grantham had known that about him his whole life.

"It doesn't," he admitted softly. "I'm sure everyone must wonder why I do not simply sack him."

Jonah shrugged. "If they do, it is because they don't understand how dangerous that could be. A man who has guarded secrets could just as easily reveal them. A double-edged sword if ever there was one."

"It seems my life is full of just those," Grantham murmured.

Jonah leaned across the desk. "Let me help you."

Grantham considered his brother-in-law carefully. Jonah had served in the Royal Navy with honor and he loved Ilaria with such a deep and abiding passion that it was impossible not to trust him.

"Actually, you may be in the perfect position to do just that. You and Ilaria do not return to London for a few weeks," Grantham mused. "What do you think of taking a small tour down to your new seat of power, my lord?"

Jonah raised both brows. "You wish for Ilaria and me to tour in the hopes it will ease the tensions?"

"No," Grantham said. "Well, yes. I'm certain that it would. Ilaria has always been deeply loved by our people and I'm sure many would like to meet you after the whirlwind in London. But it is for another purpose that I would send you. I have asked Blairford multiple times to find me a leader of this rebellion to treat with and he has all but refused."

"Refused his king?" Jonah breathed.

"He pretends that the request is impossible, but I cannot believe that to be true. I fear he has some other purpose in keeping me from this person. But you...*you* I can trust. And if there is something nefarious going on in my court, it will set off no alarm bells if you and my sister take this trip. It is official business, nothing else."

Jonah nodded. "I would be happy to do so. As I'm sure Ilaria will be. I will speak to no one but her about the true cause for the trip. Shall we plan to leave the day after Remi's wedding?"

A weight felt like it had been lifted from Grantham's shoulders. "Yes. That will be perfect. It will give staff the time to plan." He hesitated. "In fact, I'll ask Dash to lead the planning."

"You truly are mistrusting of Blairford and the other courtiers," Jonah said.

"I am. And until I can determine the truth of what is going on…I will have to be extra careful. Gather my friends and family close… perhaps my enemies closer."

Jonah gave a soft smile. "And where does Lady Ophelia fall on that measure?"

Grantham froze. "What does Lady Ophelia have to do with anything?"

"I have eyes, Your Majesty. Brother."

"They may deceive you, *Jonah*." Grantham ducked his head.

"But they don't. Come, Grantham, I saw the lady storm from your office not fifteen minutes ago, cursing and muttering to herself in a way most sailors would blush to hear. And you followed her from the parlor onto the terrace last night."

"I-I did no such thing," Grantham lied. "I needed a breath of air, I had no idea she had stepped out, herself."

"I say this with all the respect you have earned as king: bollocks."

"So none whatsoever?" Grantham asked.

Jonah laughed. "A great deal. But clearly her continued presence here is at least part of why you are…were…drinking before ten in the morning. I know a little about frustrations in love—"

"There is no love," Grantham interrupted swiftly.

Jonah stared at him for a beat too long. "Romantic entanglements, then. Whatever suits you. The point is, if you need an ear—"

"I don't." Grantham pushed to his feet and paced back to the window. Ophelia was no longer in sight, of course. But he could still picture her out in the green expanse, turning her bright blue gaze toward him. He cleared his throat. "With things as they are, I am in no position to consider a part of my future that includes, as you put it, romantic entanglements. Even if I were…to consider Lady Ophelia…"

"Why not her?"

Grantham pivoted back toward him. "Are you serious?"

"I am. She's beautiful, she's a challenge to you, which I think you like more than you let on. She's bright—"

Grantham flinched. "Yes. Too bright. Far too bright."

Jonah hesitated, and Grantham realized he had meant bright as in intelligent, which was true and a commodity that Grantham prized highly. But when bright was used as a term in conjunction with Ophelia, he couldn't help but see the sun.

Jonah seemed to recognize that, for he inclined his head as he got up from the desk. "Perhaps bright is exactly what you need then. I shall leave you and go discuss our plans with Ilaria. Then I'll reach out to Dash, as you suggested, and have him help us with the plans. Good morning."

Grantham inclined his head to dismiss Jonah, then let out a long sigh after he was gone. He feared his new brother-in-law might have hit on the material problem:

Bright was exactly what he wanted. What he craved. And that was terrifying.

CHAPTER 7

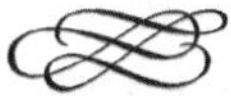

The royal wedding that had taken place in the chapel on the palace grounds such a short time before had been enormous and filled with pomp and circumstance, but this one felt even more special. Ophelia stood in the front row of the church, one of the only guests save the royals in their box to the side, and beamed as Priscilla and Remi said their vows to one another.

It was intimate and loving and just the distraction Ophelia needed after the past two frustrating days. She had barely seen Grantham in that time. He'd been holed up in his office, just passing through parlors or dining rooms. He never looked at her. And what could she say about it? She couldn't complain, even to Priscilla. Partly because her friend had been busy with wedding planning and partly because if Ophelia did vent her anger, she would also have to confess about the kiss.

And somehow that topic felt very...raw. So she'd avoided it. She'd been light and lithe and playful. When they talked, she always guided Priscilla to the topic of her wedding, steering her neatly away from the turmoil Ophelia was experiencing. Honestly, she was happy Pris wasn't sharing her room anymore. She woke so many times, sheets tangled around her, panting from dreams of Grantham's mouth on her. His hands on her.

She blinked those thoughts away now. The bishop was droning on and her gaze moved across to where the royal family was seated together. Ilaria and Sasha linked arms, their eyes brimming with happy tears as they watched Remi take his bride. Queen Giabella beamed, her gaze only shifting occasionally to where the household staff sat together, headed by her personal secretary, Dashiell Talbot.

But it was Grantham's reaction that interested her most. The king leaned forward slightly, a smile tilting his lips. A real smile, very much like the one she'd seen when he gave away his sister so recently. *There* was the man, not the king. Flesh and blood with a beating heart that actually cared about other people.

How she was drawn to that glimpse of who he really was. Who he could be.

As if he sensed her stare, he looked over at her. Their eyes locked briefly, and it was she who broke the gaze, her heart throbbing as she returned her attention to Remi and Priscilla.

The last of the vows had been spoken, Remi was placing a crown atop his wife's head and tears streamed down her face as she mouthed, *I love you.*

Ophelia flinched at that naked display of devotion. Flinched again when the couple turned and the attendees exploded in applause. Remi and Priscilla laughed together as they raced their way down the aisle, officially husband and wife. The other royals departed next and Ophelia followed them.

Outside all were gathered, the staff giving their good wishes and the family exchanging kisses and congratulations to the deliriously happy couple. Ophelia pushed away her oddly conflicted feelings as she stepped up herself, kissing Remi's cheek before Priscilla tugged her into a tight hug.

"I am so happy!" her friend whispered. She was trembling, her heart throbbing so wildly that Ophelia could feel it. "How could anyone be so happy?"

"You deserve all the happiness in the world," Ophelia said as she pulled back a fraction. "Today and all days."

"We shall walk back together," Queen Giabella announced. "And the staff is invited to join us for our celebration in the garden, as thanks for your hard work in making this wedding so beautiful in such a short time."

She sent a playfully stern look toward Remi, who gasped out a laugh. The staff stepped aside and so did Ophelia, expecting Grantham to take the queen's arm and lead the way. But before he could move to her, Giabella reached for Dashiell Talbot instead. The secretary looked surprised but pleased, and together they stepped out for the short walk back to the main palace.

Ignoring precedence, Remi and Priscilla followed behind, with Princess Ilaria and Jonah Crawford next, and Princess Sasha and Lord Bramwell after that.

Ophelia tensed as she let her gaze slip to Grantham. He shifted, muttered something beneath his breath and then approached her. "May I escort you back, my lady?" he asked, his tone laced with tension.

She steeled herself to it, ignoring her first response, which was to be defensive. Defensive wouldn't irritate him nearly as much as bouncy and light seemed to do. Let him see that how he felt about her meant nothing to her. Even if it wasn't exactly true.

"Of course, Your Majesty," she said, all but batting her eyelashes at him. "I would be delighted."

He made a gruff sound in his throat as she glided her hand into the crook of his arm. Oh dear, this was not well thought out. After all, she was very close to him. Close enough to smell the lovely spiciness of his skin, to feel the warmth of him, the firm and muscular form.

She swallowed. "It was a lovely wedding," she began. "I do not think I've ever seen any two people happier together, and I am pleased for Priscilla. After all, she's been through she very much deserves her happiness."

"I very much agree. And my brother will, shockingly, make her happiness his priority for the rest of his days, it seems."

"Shockingly?" Ophelia repeated.

"It isn't as if his reputation wasn't public knowledge," Grantham said. "Come now, my lady, we needn't play coy with each other."

She arched a brow at him. "And so you doubted he had a heart? Not particularly charitable of you."

He pursed his lips. Good, she had annoyed him. Annoying him was rather fun, though there did feel to be an edge of danger to it.

"Of course not," he said. "I have always known my brother to be more than that reputation. I did not, however, always believe he would let himself be. But he does love your friend, and I think Priscilla will be a lovely addition to our family here in Athawick. The people will like her, as well."

"Of course they will," Ophelia said. "If they do not, I will come back to Athawick myself and invade to rescue her from your clutches."

"*My* clutches?" he asked, slowing his steps and turning toward her slightly. "How will she be in my clutches?"

"Well, you are the institution, are you not, Your Majesty?" She smiled at him innocently enough. "You *are* Athawick, she is you."

She expected a huff of irritation at her point, but instead, there was a flutter that crossed his face. Something so desperate that she tightened her fingers against the inside of his elbow out of reflex. Like she could pull him back from an edge that she realized he was balanced on.

But he turned away, not responding, and their next few steps were taken in uncomfortable silence. At last she cleared her throat. "I hear that Priscilla and Remi are going to be holing up in that tower where they were secretly meeting in recent weeks."

Now he did stop and face her. "What?"

She drew back. Here she thought she had hit upon an easier topic, but it seemed not. "Did you not know?"

"No," he said. "God's teeth, Remi. There are dozens of places where they could have some privacy in these early days of their marriage. There's a wonderful cottage not three miles into the wooded area near the lake on the palace grounds. There is his own blasted room. And yet he insists on going back, over and over, to a place that was closed up for a reason."

She blinked. "What reason is that?"

He scrubbed a hand over his face and the pain reflected there, even briefly, cut her. She forgot about games and all the ways she played to irritate him. Now she edged closer and touched his hand lightly. "Not having anyone to discuss things with, personal things, is not healthy, Grantham."

He pressed his lips together, fighting. And, she thought, failing in that fight. When he let his breath out in a ragged sigh, she knew he would confess to her. And it would change things. Change them.

"My father was a reasonable king, but not a good man," he said softly. "Cruel, unyielding. I suppose *you* would say I have inherited those traits from him."

Her lips parted. "I would never say that. Ever."

His nostrils flared slightly. "He used to…lock me in that tower as punishment when I was a child."

She caught her breath at the unexpected revelation. "My God."

"It was not nearly so fine a place as Remi has created it to be for Priscilla, I can tell you that. And when I did not behave as my role, my future, should be according to my father…he would march me up the tower steps and lock me in."

"For how long?" she whispered.

"A day, sometimes two. I was allowed water and a bucket and nothing else." He turned his face. "No one knew. Not my mother, not my brother."

"I would hope not," she said softly. "Or using that place for a romantic assignation would seem especially cruel. How old were you?"

He hesitated. "Ten the first time. Fifteen the last."

She squeezed her eyes shut. "So young."

"Old enough to know better, he used to say," Grantham said, just as softly as she had spoken, but his tone was raw. Rough. He shook his head. "I should not have said anything to you. Forgive me for my imprudence. I must catch up with the others and speak to Remi."

He pivoted away, stalking off as she stared. He had revealed something of himself and now she knew the truth. There *was* a man in there, buried beneath propriety and hard edges and cold civility. The man who had kissed her, who still stung from the abusive treatment of a father. A man with weight on his shoulders and no outlet to release it.

Except to grunt and demand and march across rooms to confront. As he apparently intended to do with Remi at that moment. She raced forward, rushing after him. He would not feel better by berating his brother. Priscilla would be upset. And if no one knew what he had endured, it would only serve to create a further wedge between Grantham and his family.

One she felt driven to keep from happening. Even though it was most certainly not her place.

❦

Grantham's hands were shaking and his ears were ringing as he started around the perimeter of the palace toward the garden in the back. Even from the distance he could hear the laughter of those gathered in celebration and it made him slow his steps. Should he approach Remi after all? Confront him about the tower?

Usually he wouldn't question himself, but at this moment Ophelia was in his head. Bouncing around where she certainly didn't belong, making him question...everything. She made him question everything.

How could one slender slip of a woman upend an entire life? That was the question. He spent five minutes with her and he was flipped onto his head. Kiss her? He would never be the same. And he couldn't afford those changes, those cracks to a façade that he had built up so carefully over the years.

More to the point, he didn't *want* them. He didn't want to give any other person in the world such vulnerability. That was exactly how a person ended up in a tower…one in a palace or in one's own head.

"Your Majesty!"

He slowed in his steps a little. Ophelia was following him.

"Sir!"

He ignored her.

"Grantham!" she called out at last.

That stopped him, with all its impertinence and familiarity. He pivoted to glare at her. They were alongside the palace now, just out of view of the gardens.

"What do you want, Ophelia?" he barked, and then fisted his hands at his sides. "For God's sake, woman. What do you want?"

The second question came out softer, almost in defeat and that wasn't wrong. He felt a little defeated as she moved to him, blue eyes bright with warmth and a hint of what he feared was pity.

"Please reconsider speaking to Remi and Priscilla about the tower," she said.

He blinked. "Why do you bloody care? Or is it just that you want to continue your current pastime of tweaking me, despite my position, that drives you to intrude where you do not belong?"

Her lips parted slightly, but she didn't flinch away. She never did that, did she? She always stood toe to toe with him, never breaking first, always a challenge. Bait he kept rising to even though he should be better. But he *liked* to match with her. He liked to stand next to her.

He liked to touch her. He wanted to touch her even now.

"I belong no less than you do in this situation," she insisted, firmly but not unkindly. "I understand that the tower has a deeply painful association for you. And I am sorry that someone was so cruel to you when you were helpless to escape. That was wrong and

I don't care if your father was king of a country or head fishmonger. Cruelty is cruelty, even if it wears a crown."

He blinked. He had not expected that understanding. "But?" he pressed.

"But you said that Remi does not know about what happened to you there," she said gently. "To him and Priscilla, that place is an oasis, a place where they discovered their love. It is a beautiful escape. Do you want to take that from them? Or couldn't you see that as a way that the tower has been…cleansed a little from your pain?"

He pursed his lips. When he realized Remi was using the tower, the tower Grantham had ordered locked, never to be opened again, he had burned with rage. Only the drama that had followed with Priscilla's horrible parents had tempered it. But he could see now, through Ophelia's eyes, how unfair that reaction was. He was angry at his father, not his brother.

"You think I would steal some of their happiness," he said softly.

She nodded. "And they wouldn't understand why."

"He would just see me as cruel," he said slowly. "As bad as our father."

She moved closer, and once again she caught his hand. He hated that she wore gloves. He wanted to feel her skin against his as he had when he kissed her.

"Despite our differences, I have said it once and I will say it again: you are not cruel. Stern. Unreadable. Frustrating." His lips quirked at her directness. "But never cruel."

He let out a long breath. "I won't intrude upon their day."

Her grip tightened on his hand. "Thank you, Grantham," she said, her voice just above a whisper. "Thank you."

He should have stepped away. Every reasonable part of him told him that he had to do so. To separate from this woman who was the most beautiful ball of chaos and sunshine he had ever met. The woman who could destroy all he had built, knock down his walls so effortlessly. That was danger.

And yet he didn't step back. Instead he pulled her closer. Her breath hitched as she stared up at him, her gaze going a little unfocused as it trailed to his mouth and then swiftly back again. He felt her tremble. He trembled too as her skirt made a swish against his boots.

He lifted the hand she didn't hold, opening the fist that had made his knuckles white and gliding the fingers along her impossibly soft cheek. She turned into his touch, the smallest sigh escaping her lips.

He leaned in, unable to stop now, the voice of reason fading to nothingness, replaced by raw and powerful desire. He felt her breath on his lips just before they touched, and it was like someone turned off control. He drowned in that sensation as he claimed her mouth for the second time in a handful of days.

She opened to him immediately and he delved into the pleasure of her taste: sweet like tea, warm like a bath, powerful like a wave on the ocean that could drag him out to sea. He welcomed it all, wrapping his arms around her, pulling her against him so that her curves molded against his and her whimper was lost on his tongue.

She met him stroke for stroke. There was no simpering or withdrawing or questioning in the way she kissed him back. She knew what she wanted. She knew what *he* wanted. Despite their often contentious relationship, she seemed more than willing to give and receive both. And it would be so fucking easy to take what he wanted. To push her back into the shadow of the palace wall. To run his hands all over her body until she was shaking, begging. To align their bodies and take until they were soaked in each other's sweat and shaking with merged pleasure.

It would be too easy to do that. To forget himself.

That was her power.

He stepped away, releasing her gently so she wouldn't lose her balance. He shook his head. "This cannot happen."

She blinked at him, lips swollen and wet from his mouth. "It just did."

He bent his head. "You...you like to play, Ophelia. You like to dance in the light and tempt the stars. And that's wonderful. Infuriating, but wonderful." He waved toward the garden in the distance, toward the sounds of those gathered there. "I *can't* play. So this has to stop."

He didn't wait for her response, but turned away and started toward the garden instead. But as he walked, he heard her say one word. It echoed in the air and would echo in his mind for a long time to come.

"Coward."

He froze and didn't look back even as he said, "Probably."

Then he kept walking back to his subjects, back to his life, back to the emptiness that was the only way for him to stay afloat in the storm.

CHAPTER 8

"I'm so sorry to intrude."

Ophelia glanced up from the book she had been reading, curled up on a comfortable window seat in the glorious library. She was surprised to find the queen, herself, at the door, hands clasped as she awaited Ophelia's response.

Queen Giabella was a beautiful woman, with dark hair and eyes that most of her children, save Remi, had inherited. She was sophisticated—no one who didn't know her role would have ever been surprised to be told she was a queen—but she was also kind. There was a genuineness to her that permeated from every look and word.

Ophelia hustled to her feet and executed a small curtsey. "Not at all, Your Majesty. May I be of some service?"

Queen Giabella stepped into the room. "I was about to go into the garden and cut roses for some centerpieces for an event later in the day. My daughters are both busy with their husbands, as is Priscilla, so I realized it would offer me the perfect opportunity to make your acquaintance on a more personal level."

Ophelia swallowed hard. She wasn't sure that was the best of ideas. After all, it had been nearly two days since Grantham's searing kiss after the wedding. The man had ignored and avoided her since. He probably wouldn't want her any nearer his mother any more than he wanted her near him.

Defiance won over uncertainty, as well as the desire to know the queen better. "Of course, Your Majesty. Will I need a spencer, do you think?" She glanced down at her short-sleeved gown.

"No, it is unseasonably warm this afternoon." The queen beckoned for her and they walked from the library and up the hallway together.

They exited the palace and down the veranda stairs into the garden. Two baskets and two pairs of cutters and gloves awaited them at the entrance to the garden, and Ophelia smiled as she tugged the gloves on. "You do prepare for everything."

"Our staff is truly the best." The queen's smile fluttered slightly. "On the whole. Now, what do you think for centerpieces?"

"I suppose it depends on the event," Ophelia said as they made their way to the rows of rose bushes.

"The king is hosting a few of his ministers and a handful of aristocrats from various parts of the island. Save Jonah, of course, as he and Ilaria have gone to visit his new seat in the south for a few days. You are welcome to join us, of course. The dignitaries will probably welcome a fresh face and not *all* of them are terrible bores."

There was something about the queen's tone that made Ophelia examine her more carefully. Though she hid it under smiles and calm rather than Grantham's frowns and storms, she looked as concerned as the king. Best to proceed carefully, it seemed.

"Of course I will join if you'd like, Your Majesty. It sounds as though the gathering is great importance. I think the bold red, to make a statement of strength, don't you think?" Ophelia asked, beckoning to the roses.

"I agree. But perhaps with some hints of white, for peace," the queen suggested.

"Perfect."

The queen gave some instruction on approximate numbers and then they stepped up to the bushes together, each carefully choosing blooms for the purpose. It was quiet for a short while, with both of them focusing on the task at hand. However, Ophelia felt the queen's gaze shift to her from time to time, felt the questions bubbling up in her.

And since she wasn't sure how she could answer certain questions, she decided to take the reins herself. "You are from Everlay, are you not, Your Majesty?"

The queen arched a brow, as if she realized Ophelia was making the first move in a chess game. But she nodded. "I am. A very small nation, but then again, so is Athawick. But our locations on trade routes have made both countries important. Important enough to link our nations through marriage."

Ophelia thought of Grantham's brief recounting of his troubled relationship with the previous king. "You always knew you would marry King Alistair?"

Queen Giabella pivoted slightly toward her. "Ah, you have studied your history to know my husband's name. Most in London did not, for they only think of Athawick when we make an official visit."

"I have," Ophelia said. "I thought it would only be polite if coming to your country to know a little about it. Though it seems there is always more."

"Yes, even after nearly thirty-five years in this country, I always find new tidbits of history. An ever-opening rose like this one," the queen said, holding up a perfect bloom she had just cut before she placed it in her basket with the others. "And yes, I always knew. Our fathers arranged the match when we were just children."

Ophelia blinked as a terrible thought entered her mind. "And does King Grantham also have an arrangement in the wings?"

Giabella hesitated before she clipped the next rose. "He does not. The last arrangement was fruitful, but not particularly…happy, I will admit. I convinced Alistair that we should at least wait to arrange marriages until the children were old enough to have a say.

A plan that did not exactly work correctly when it came to Ilaria, though I am happy for her choice and her joy."

Ophelia smiled. Everyone knew the story of the princess's defiance of the match that had been chosen for her, and of her adopted sister Sasha's marriage to the Earl of Bramwell instead.

"You are curious about Grantham's choices, it seems," Giabella said softly.

Ophelia clipped a bloom and cleared her throat. "I suppose everyone is. It isn't that kings don't visit London often enough, but hardly any of them are young as he is. Or handsome." She blinked as she realized what she'd said. "Or so many people think."

"But not you?" the queen asked with a laugh.

Oh dear, now Ophelia was really mucking this up entirely. "Of course he is handsome. That is a fact, not a question. I only mean that some young ladies in London, and I'm sure here in Athawick, were interested in his prospects. He does not seem in a hurry to find his match like his brother and sisters have done, though."

"He has a great deal of weight on his shoulders at present." Again Giabella seemed faraway as she spoke. Tense. "A partner, the right partner, could ease that burden. But he is as stubborn as… well, he's stubborn. He will only decide his future when he is ready. And I learned my lesson with his siblings not to interfere too much."

Ophelia nodded and then glanced up at the palace. She found the study window too easily, and thought she saw a shadow of a person there. The king? Watching her. Just as he always seemed to be. The shadow moved, and she sighed.

She needed to get out of this dangerous territory. "Priscilla and Prince Remington seem a very good match."

The queen eyed her for a moment but then graciously allowed for the subject change. The rest of the time they worked in the garden, they spoke of other topics, not Grantham. And yet he was all Ophelia thought about. And she could not help but continue to glance up at his window and wonder if he were there, standing out of view, thinking of her, too. Despite his best efforts to avoid her and whatever was brewing between them.

~

"And how do you like having your palace back, Your Majesty?" Grantham blinked and brought his attention back to Count Friskar of the Northern Realm of the island. He had never had a problem with the man, who was about ten years older than Grantham and had only recently inherited the title from his father, a crony of the past king.

"Though your remaining houseguest seems charming, indeed."

Grantham followed Friskar's knowing smile toward Ophelia across the room. She was standing with the other attending counts, the center of their collective attention as she chatted about what, he could not guess. Something that seemed to light up every man within ten feet of her.

"Charming," he grunted. "That is one way of putting it. My mother asked her to join the party, it seems."

He had no way of confronting the queen about it, of course. It seemed the right thing to do from a distance, for Ophelia was very good at capturing the attention of anyone around her. She was an entertainment to a bunch of stuffy men who were tired of each other's company after so much of it over the years.

And yet Grantham was not eased by her presence. No, he had been studiously avoiding her for days, trying to make his mind stop pivoting endlessly on the kisses they'd shared. Having her in the same room as him only started all his longing up again. Frayed all his careful control.

As if she sensed that weakness, she flitted her gaze away from her companions and instead met his eyes. She didn't blush or look away, she just held there. Bold. Direct. All the heat in his body felt like it slid southward, and for probably the first time in his life he was happy for the more voluminous robes of his full formal outfit, for it covered the reaction his body made despite the inopportune timing.

"Your Majesty?"

He shook off his thoughts as he realized Friskar had spoken to him again. "Woolgathering, my apologies. What were you saying?"

"I was just wondering if you had more information regarding the situation in the south."

Whatever pleasure that had been engendered in him by looking at Ophelia, as unwanted as it had been, fled in an instant at the reminder of his precarious position. "The new count and my sister are on their way to observe the situation in person," he admitted. "I had hoped that time would mute the unrest, as all settled into the new routine of a fresh face holding the crown."

"And yet it hasn't." Friskar was direct, as was his look. "I will tell you, sir, that as the protests against you become louder all over the island, some of the other aristocrats are beginning to...to whisper about your handling of this situation."

Grantham set his legs a bit wider, almost physically preparing for this attack. "The others, or you?"

"I'm not as attached to my power, I suppose," Friskar said with a shrug. "I'm telling you as...an ally. A friend, insomuch as you can have those."

Grantham all but physically forced his shoulders to relax. "And I thank you for it. I also give you my promise that the problems are being taken seriously by the crown. They will be resolved..." He trailed off as he thought of how Blairford and the other courtiers, how some of the counts, how some of his other advisors, wished to resolve the issue. His stomach turned.

"If I can be of assistance," Friskar said, "please let me know."

Grantham inclined his head, but his attention was drawn yet again as he watched Ophelia excuse herself from the company of the others and slowly make her way across the parlor. She hesitated at the door and gave him a quick look over her shoulder. Then she was gone.

"Thank you," Grantham said, dragging himself back to his companion. "I appreciate it. Will you excuse me?"

Friskar nodded and Grantham stepped away, toward where Ophelia had gone. He hesitated, unable to see her now that she had gone up the hall. He had no business seeking her out when this room was filled with allies and enemies alike. Some poised to choose which side they fell on.

But all he could think about was where in the world Ophelia was going. And with a quick glance at the room, he followed her, even though he knew it was the wrong answer to a question he refused to acknowledge and yet couldn't deny. Couldn't escape.

A question that could destroy his kingdom, his future, and most of all…his heart.

CHAPTER 9

Ophelia drew her fingertips along the fine wallpaper as she moved up the hall away from the parlor. She hadn't been able to spend one more moment in that stuffy room with those stuffy men. They were all sniffing after her. That was nothing new. Men had been seeking her since before she'd even come out in Society.

But they were also all watching Grantham, just as she had been. Only they wanted him to fail. She saw it on their faces, heard it in the tones of their voices and the knowing quality of their questions.

And oh, how she had wanted to rush to his defense. To tear those men to shreds. But it wasn't her place. It would only cause more consternation for the very man she felt oddly compelled to protect.

If Grantham's pained expression had been any indication, he didn't need more of that. She knew she caused enough of it by her very existence in his home. She played it up, didn't she? Making it all a game. Enticing him to play it, sometimes against his will.

She sighed as her fingers brushed against the tall double doors that led into the throne room. She paused. She had been here for Jonah Crawford's investiture as count a few weeks before, but the room was not open usually. This was Grantham's true domain, though. His seat of power.

And she found herself testing the large brass handles. To her surprise, the door creaked open and she held her breath as she stepped inside.

It was quiet in the cavernous room. The shades were almost all drawn, though one had been done so hastily, it seemed, for a shaft of bright sunshine tumbled across the room. It landed, very artistically, on the throne which sat on a low stage just up a short set of three shallow stairs.

She was drawn to it, but did not go to the throne instantly. Instead she made her way around the outside edge of the room, taking in all the details of the room. There were stern portraits of previous kings hung along the walls. Watching and judging their successors. She felt it just looking up at the paintings. She had to believe Grantham felt the same every time he entered this room.

Perhaps every time he entered *any* room.

In the corner of the chamber there was a huge cabinet with a glass face. Inside there were swords mounted—ceremonial, it seemed—and a very pompous crown with a high blue cloth cap with sewn bejeweled stars in the center. She couldn't imagine Grantham wearing such a thing. He looked fine in the burnished silver crown he had worn today, but this ornamental one seemed too…too *silly* for such a serious and studious person.

She stepped aside, coming closer to the throne with each step. There was another small chair set behind the main throne. Someone had explained to her that it was for the queen. Not whoever Grantham would marry, for she would take a place right beside him, but for his mother.

Right now, though, his throne was the lonely center of the dais. She hesitated before she climbed the short stairs and stood before the chair. It was made from some kind of gray, weathered wood and carved intricately with the same animals that graced the Athawickian flag: swans and whales all turned toward an intricate sun across the top of the throne.

The seat was lined with a blue velvet cushion and it was twice as wide as a normal chair might be. Two people might be able to fit if they were small enough. Even for Grantham, who was a large man, there would be ample room around him to take any position, sprawled or formal.

The idea of him sprawled here made her heart throb a little faster.

She drew in an unsteady breath as she touched the armrests of the seat with both hands. She leaned over it, thinking of the many men who had taken this place. Of the one who took it now.

Her knees had begun to shake, and she turned and slowly sank into position in the throne. *His* seat, which felt like it engulfed her in that moment. The wave of responsibility washed over her and she gasped for breath at the feel of it. She folded her hands in her lap and stared out at the dozens of empty chairs, all that pomp and circumstance put away but only just below the surface. If this room were full, she could imagine this view of it would be more than intimidating.

She was about to get up again when the doors to the throne room burst open. She caught her breath and watched as Grantham, himself, stepped into the room. His gaze scanned across the room and finally settled on her.

Even across the room, even in the dim light, she saw the flicker of emotion move across his face. Frustration and anguish, envy and desire, all tangled in one ever-moving expression that was focused on her. Only on and only for her. The spark that had flashed between them, that she had denied and ignored and, if she were honest with herself, tried to flame, roared to life.

His nostrils flared slightly as he yanked the doors shut behind him, closing them in together in the huge, quiet, entirely private room. When he charged across the room toward her like a bull, she wasn't afraid. Because she could see he wasn't actually angry. No, he was something else entirely. Something heated and powerful and mesmerizing.

"Get up," he said, soft but firm.

She ought to have done just that. Sitting in his throne was entirely inappropriate. And yet she just couldn't stop…baiting him. That was the way to bring him close, after all. Bait and catch, catch and release, bait again…

She slowly shook her head no and stayed exactly where she was.

He skidded to a stop about three strides away from her and stared at her, almost comically confused that she would refuse him. "Ophelia."

She said nothing in response, just continued to stare down at him from the dais. He crossed the three strides, came up one step and now his face was even with hers. He leaned in, bracing one hand on each of the throne's armrests.

He was so close now. A breath away as he repeated, "Get up."

This time he said it slowly, succinctly. Her heart was pounding and her palms actually itched in her lap. She wanted to touch him, wanted to rake her nails across his shoulders, wanted to make him break. What would he look like if he broke and all the constrained passion raged free?

She didn't do it. Instead she arched a brow and was happy her voice didn't tremble too much when she said, "Or what?"

His nostrils flared again, and oh, yes, she saw the frustration she provoked in him. She also saw so much more. His pupils had dilated, his breath was a little shorter, he couldn't stop dropping his focused gaze to her mouth, so close and yet far too far.

But he was still the king. She saw the king there in his eyes, too. The part of him that would insist on keeping his distance. On stopping this storm that seemed to stir up the moment they were within any distance of each other.

She didn't *want* the king. The king was an institution, a thought, a theory.

No, she wanted the man. Only the man. And a wicked, wicked

thought passed through her mind. One she couldn't deny, or didn't choose to deny at any rate. She lifted her hand toward him. He tracked her fingers, shuddering slightly when she brushed just the tips of them across his cheek, reveling in the roughness of his short-trimmed beard.

She moved higher, tangling them into his thick hair where she caught the crown still perched on his head. Gently, careful not to yank any of that hair free, she lifted the crown away.

He stopped breathing entirely, his eyes wide as she started to lower the crown. He caught her wrist, not in a painful grip, but certainly it wasn't a gentle one either. She waited, unspeaking, unmoving, unwavering as she held his gaze. The room was shrinking now, spiraling down to only them, so close together.

"Ophelia," he whispered again, this time almost a plea.

She refused to answer it. He didn't release her wrist, but instead used his opposite hand to take the crown from her fingers. She expected him to put it on again, but instead he raised it up, hanging it on one of the ears of the throne where it dangled, swinging gently and making a light tap against the wood.

Then his fingers cupped her face and he was kissing her. Hard and fast, with more passion than he had allowed the last two times this had happened. He drove into her, forceful, demanding, and she met him stroke for stroke. He released her wrist and she wrapped both arms around his shoulders, opening her legs so he could lean in closer, bunching the fabric from her skirts around his body.

His fingers clenched at her back, molding her even closer until the heat between them began to feel combustible. She arched against him, her entire body pulsing with a desire unlike any she'd experienced in the past. Something animal and hungry that spread throughout her entire being, heating her every limb, settling to throb between her legs. She wanted this man. Wanted him so much that she could taste it on her tongue as much as she tasted him.

He dragged his mouth away, down the side of her throat, sucking there as she gasped in pleasure. His hands slid lower, cupping her hips, sliding her forward to the edge of the throne and tightening her skirts around her body even more.

One hand slid down the outside line of her leg, the pressure firm and warm through the fabric of her gown. He bunched the dress into his fist, tugging it up as he went, until her legs were exposed. Then he touched her stockinged thigh, and she cried out with surprise and pleasure. God, his hands. His hands were like fire against her. She wanted them to touch her bare skin, she wanted them to cradle her against him as he took her.

He dropped to his knees on the stairs, moving his mouth lower over her still-clothed breast. Down over her stomach.

"Please," she gasped, lifting into him shamelessly, seeking pleasure she had only ever found with her own hand but instinctively knew he would provide in ways she probably hadn't yet imagined.

He glanced up at her. His gaze was almost entirely black with desire, his expression hungry and heated. There was no king there anymore, just a man who had been denying himself for far too long. A man who would not deny himself now. Couldn't.

He shoved the skirt the rest of the way up, bunching it around her stomach. Now he could open her legs, and he did, shouldering his way between them. She stared down at him, dizzied by what she saw. On his knees he looked like he was there to be knighted by her. Or to worship her.

All thoughts of any kind exited her mind when he slid his hands up the inside of her thighs, along the soft fabric of her drawers. When he reached the apex, he hesitated and then slowly tugged the slit in them open wide. She felt the blood rush to her cheeks as he stared at her sex. The moment stretched so long she feared he might come to his senses and back away. But instead, he glanced up at her, licked his lips and then bent between her legs.

He tugged at the slit in her drawers, tearing the fabric at the seam so it opened even wider. She felt the steam of his breath against the sensitive flesh and rocked toward him with a moan. One that elevated when he actually pressed his mouth to her.

Ophelia had once upon a time found a very naughty book that described this act, but she had never experienced it. She found herself happy because having this man be the first was something special. He licked her, at first very gently, tracing her length with his tongue and letting loose a rumble of pleasure deep in his chest. She found herself lifting into him, seeking what he was giving, seeking more.

He didn't deny her. Slowly those licks became harder. He feasted on her, tasting every fold of her body, drawing her farther open with his thumbs to delve even deeper into her wet flesh. The sensation was unbelievable, like electric pleasure that pulsed from wherever he touched her and ricocheted through her entire being.

She writhed on the throne, gripping the armrests with both hands, grinding against his tongue as he began to focus the flick of it against her clitoris. Faster, harder, until the waves of pleasure mounted and her vision blurred. Still, he never let her fall over the edge, never allowed her to find the release she needed. Not until he sucked.

He sucked her clitoris and the world tipped on its side as her body began to pulse in hard, heavy, fantastic waves of sensation. She sat up straighter, gripping his head in both hands, pulsing against his tongue as she gasped and cried out in the quiet of the room. He dragged her through the sensation, pushing her just to the edge of pain before he finally withdrew his mouth from her body and rocked back to look at her.

It was silent for what felt like forever. At first he looked pleased, smug even as he took in the slick evidence of his handiwork. But then it was as if he woke up. Like he came back into himself at last and realized what he had done. Where he had done it.

"Grantham," she whispered as the horror entered his stare.

She reached for him, but he stood up in one fluid unfolding of muscle and sinew, wiping her from his beard with the back of his hand. She could see the outline of his hard cock against his trousers before the robes of his formal garment fell to conceal it.

He didn't answer, only shoved a hand through his hair. He looked down at her, still sprawled on his throne, sex surely glistening in the thin beam of light that highlighted her. He held up a hand, as if to touch her, as if to ward her off.

Then he turned and left the room without another word.

She stood, smoothing her gown back down over herself. Her body still pulsed with the pleasure he had created. The warmth that spread through every part of her in a way it never had before.

And yet she wasn't happy. No, she was wrecked. She had looked into his eyes and seen so much pain, so much regret, so much self-recrimination that she feared this would end whatever they'd just begun. For the first time she realized she didn't *want* that to end. She wanted to explore the tension that always existed between them.

She wanted more of him, more of this, more of everything. And maybe that was the problem. For a man like him, this was too much. *She* was too much. And she'd never disliked that fact more.

CHAPTER 10

Grantham didn't remember leaving the throne room. He didn't remember moving through the halls or mounting the steps to the tower he'd hated most of his life. He just found himself at the door there, staring at the barrier, his hand lifted to knock.

Or had he already knocked? There was movement inside the chamber like he had and the occupants were pulling themselves together to answer.

"It's me," he said, and he hardly recognized his own voice. It sounded so...hollow. "I...I need to talk to Remi."

The key turned in the lock from the other side of the door and then opened. Remi was in his trousers, but was shirtless. Behind him, Grantham saw Priscilla, wrapped up in a robe, her hair mussed. Obviously he had interrupted. Normally he would have just excused himself, but right now...he couldn't.

"I just need..." he began.

Remi's brow wrinkled and he caught Grantham's arm, pulling him into the chamber. "You look like you've just seen a ghost. What is it? Is Mama well?"

"She's fine," Grantham assured him. "I'm sorry to interrupt, Priscilla."

She shook her head. "Don't trouble yourself. I think there is a bath waiting in the other room. Perhaps I'll avail myself of that while you two talk." She sent Remi a meaningful look and then slipped away, shutting the door to the dressing room section of the chamber.

"I assume that was meant to be a bath for two," Grantham said, ducking his head and wishing his mind didn't conjure images of Ophelia in a bath waiting for *him*. "I apologize for ruining your fun."

"No one can ruin my fun, I assure you. Sometimes the waiting is the best part." Remi tilted his head. "What is wrong with you?"

"I'm so obvious?" Grantham asked, unsure of how to start now that he was here, so he decided to stall instead.

"You know you are," Remi said. "You hate this tower. I've never understood why. You wouldn't come up here without a reason."

Grantham swallowed. No, no one knew why he hated this tower. Except Ophelia. He'd told Ophelia his secret, hadn't he? Opened up to her unlike he'd ever done with anyone, not for years. And then defiled her in his throne room.

He shivered at the thought of her sprawled on the seat, legs wide, sex slick from his tongue and her orgasm. He could still taste her. How could one be so aroused and hate oneself so much all at the same time?

"Grantham!"

He jolted at Remi's sharp tone. "I'm sorry. I just…I didn't know where else to go. Who else to talk to. Who else would ever understand what I've…what I've done."

Remi's brow knitted with concern and he motioned to one of the chairs before the fire. "Sit."

Grantham wasn't accustomed to being ordered about, and under normal circumstances he might have bristled, but in this moment he was pleased to have someone else direct him. He was clearly incapable of directing himself.

He sat and Remi snatched up a discarded shirt from the end of the rumpled bed. As he pulled it over his head, he said, "Speak."

Grantham ran a hand through his hair. "I kissed Ophelia."

Remi sat down across from him, and from the expression on his face, Grantham could see he was less than impressed with this confession. "So? I'm honestly surprised it took this long, I noticed your attraction to the woman weeks ago. You can't take your eyes off her and—"

"Not on the lips," Grantham said, cutting off whatever his brother would have said next.

Remi stared at him, expression blank and unreadable for what felt like a lifetime. "Ah, you *kissed* Ophelia."

Grantham nodded. "In the throne room. On Father's throne. My throne? *The* throne."

Remi's eyes went impossibly wide and he leaned forward. "I'm sorry, what did you do?"

Grantham jumped to his feet. "All she does is lure me with those ridiculous eyes. She taunts and teases and tempts and then she spreads this light across everything she does. I can't chase that, I don't have the freedom you and our sisters have had to do so. And yet here she is, like a rainbow through the gloom. After the first time I kissed her—"

"You've done this multiple times?" Remi burst out.

"Not that kind of kiss. A kiss-kiss. A regular kiss. Lip to lip." Grantham huffed. "After the first time, I told myself I couldn't repeat it. After the second time I told *her* the same. But it's like I can't stop myself. It's magnetic, this attraction. So much so that I forget my place, forget my limitations. Forget where I am."

Remi let out a breath slowly. "I still don't understand how you ended up in the throne room."

"I followed her. I just left in the middle of the gathering with the counts and the advisors, stalked off like my main duty isn't to my country, as if my position isn't being threatened at every turn. I left all that to follow a woman. And instead of kicking her out of the room, instead of insisting she stand up off of the throne and stop... stop *tempting* me, I dropped to my knees and...and..."

He stopped himself and shut his eyes. He could still hear Ophelia's gasp of pleasure, the soft moans, the way she said *please* and broke him at last.

"What did I do?" he whispered.

Remi wrinkled his brow. "The amount of guilt you are expressing is not equal to what you've done."

"On the *throne*, Remi," Grantham said, tilting his head.

Remi lifted his brows. "It's quite impressive, really. I wish I'd thought of it."

Despite himself, Grantham felt a smile tug the edges of his mouth. He fought it admirably and shook his head. "Stop."

Remi moved toward him. "You're acting like you're English. We don't see sex with such a ridiculous view that they do. So why torment yourself so?"

Throwing up his hands, Grantham said, "Because *she* is English and they definitely value virginity in a way we don't. What I've done would be considered ruination. And certainly it must have shocked her."

She hadn't seemed shocked, but that didn't mean anything. She had been swept away like he was, but he couldn't imagine what she thought now. What questions had been hatched in her mind.

He would have pondered it more, but he noticed that Remi's expression changed, just in the slightest and his gaze darted away. Like he knew a secret.

"What is that look?" Grantham demanded. "Remi?"

"It is not my secret to tell," his brother said. "I wasn't even told it, frankly. Just guessed."

Grantham's eyes went wide. Remi had changed when he mentioned the topic of virginity. "Are you implying that Ophelia is not a virgin?"

Remi would know, he supposed, because he and Priscilla didn't seem to keep secrets. What that would be like, he couldn't even imagine.

"I haven't *said* anything," Remi said slowly. "Christ, Grantham, your ability to see through everyone is quite a thing. Why don't you talk to Ophelia about what happened? About what she wants? For all you know, it might even be more."

Grantham's stomach flipped at that thought. "More? What makes you think *I* want more?"

"Because I can also see through you, you arse." Remi smiled at him gently. "Mostly. I can see how much you're struggling, even if you refuse to let anyone in. And I can see how much you want this woman every time you look at her. She is here so short a time, why not allow yourself pleasure if she wants the same? At the very least, it might ease some of this tension. Make her less of a distraction if you are no longer trying to avoid her."

Grantham considered that. It was true that most of his intruding thoughts about Ophelia were of the vein of fantasy. His dreams about her heated and powerful. If he did go to her, come to some arrangement about her remaining time in Athawick…certainly the shine would come off, wouldn't it? It would be reality and he could sort that out, pack it away when he needed to. He'd been doing it his whole life.

"I…I should speak to her," he admitted slowly. "Oh, how the mighty have fallen that I am taking advice from you."

Remi grinned. "I know. I'm shocked at it, myself." He nudged Grantham lightly. "Good on you, mate."

Grantham rolled his eyes at his brother's enthusiasm for his shockingly bad behavior. "Please don't act like this was a good thing."

"Did you enjoy yourself?"

Grantham blinked, memories of the sweetness of Ophelia's flavor, the clench of her thighs around him, the way she'd gasped out pleasure against his tongue all bombarded him. "Yes."

"And did she?"

Once again, he thought of how her body had flexed against him, the powerful waves of orgasm rocking him down to his very core. "Yes."

"Then it wasn't a bad thing, at the very least," Remi said.

Grantham sighed. He wasn't certain Remi was entirely correct in that assessment. At least not yet. "I will let you get back to your wife." He turned and moved toward the door, but stopped there and turned back. "I...I'm glad I spoke to you about this."

Remi's expression softened and it warmed Grantham. They had been so close as boys, but recent years had pulled them further and further apart. To the point that Remi had actually hit him just a few days before. But in this moment, he felt their bond of brotherhood strengthen once again.

"So am I," Remi said.

Grantham nodded and then left the room. After he shut the door, he leaned against it briefly, trying to calm his racing heart and find his breath again. This was clearly not the right moment to find Ophelia, not when he was still teetering on the edge of control.

So he would go work. And plan his next move with the woman who seemed to test his restraint without even trying.

~

Ophelia stared at her plate as she pushed the food on it around with the tines of her fork. She had hardly eaten any of the delicious delicacies, including lobster caught fresh that day by Athawickian fisherman.

But how could one eat when Grantham was sitting at the head of the table five places away, talking to one of the visiting counts as if nothing had happened between them just a few hours before? Did it mean nothing to him?

But no, she knew that wasn't true. She glanced up and looked at him directly. He glanced her way like he felt her regard and his cheek twitched slightly, his pupils dilated. She moved him. What had happened moved him. He was simply better at hiding it.

Which left her wondering what the hell would come out of it? Would he simply never speak of it again? Never speak to *her* again?

Would the moment be repeated, perhaps when the tension between them reached a boiling point again? Or would he avoid her so that his façade of control would never be cracked again?

"Ophelia?"

She jolted as Priscilla, who had been seated next to her, placed a gentle hand on hers. She forced a smile for her friend. "Yes?"

Priscilla's brow wrinkled with worry. "Are you well?"

Ophelia cleared her throat and shifted to a straighter position in her chair. "Of course. I'm fit as a fiddle."

"Very believable when you start speaking in idioms."

Ophelia barely resisted the urge to stick out her tongue at her friend. Priscilla did know her too well. And Ophelia wasn't trying to keep what had happened a secret—she just had to think on it more before she confessed what she had done with Grantham. Ophelia couldn't help but wonder if she would be censured, especially considering her troubled past. Her lapses in judgment.

"I see you aren't going to beat around the bush," Ophelia said.

Priscilla giggled. "Stop it now."

"Better late than never," Ophelia offered. It seemed the playfulness had distracted her friend and that was a good thing.

"You are terrible," Priscilla said as she raised her napkin to control her laughter. "But I mean the question. You are pale and distracted."

Ophelia pursed her lips. Damn. She hadn't distracted Pris as much as she thought she had. "I'm fine," she said, and felt the lie of it. "I promise."

"You can talk to me," Priscilla said softly, and there was a tone to her voice that made Ophelia look closer. Priscilla had never been very good at covering up her thoughts or feelings. Her expressive face revealed all, and in that moment it seemed like she...she knew. She knew something had happened.

Ophelia caught her breath. How would Pris know? Unless... unless Grantham had said something to Remi, and Remi had told her. Could that be true?

"Ophelia," Priscilla said, and squeezed her hand tighter.

"I will talk to you," Ophelia promised, and meant it. "I will. I'm just not ready yet."

"I understand that," Priscilla said with a sigh. "Just…be careful."

Ophelia nodded, and then they were distracted as one of the counts turned his attention to them. She pushed her thoughts away and spoke politely to the man about her time in Athawick. The interruption was a relief, really, and the rest of the supper she found herself able to concentrate a bit better. As long as she didn't look at Grantham and ponder the heavenly feeling of his tongue against her body, it was fine. Everything was fine.

Eventually, the supper ended. Grantham escorted his mother to the parlor; his sister Sasha was taken by her husband, the Earl of Bramwell; Remi and Priscilla went together. The very count Ophelia had been talking to offered his arm. He was older than she by several years, but not an unpleasant man. He spoke of crops a bit too much, but she welcomed the benign topic when her mind raced so completely.

In the sitting room, Grantham's distancing from her continued. After half an hour, she had all but accepted that he would not speak to her about what had happened.

As if he knew it, that was the moment Grantham chose to step away from the dignitary he had been speaking to and move toward her. She tensed as he reached her and inclined his head with all politeness and correctness.

"My lady," he said.

She offered a brief curtsey. "Your Majesty."

He stood beside her, and they were quiet a moment. There was no comfort to the silence, though, and she feared he could likely hear her heart pounding in her chest.

"I…I think we need to talk," he said at last, turning toward her. "Alone."

She stared up at him with his unreadable expression. God's

teeth, why did he make this so hard? Why couldn't he give her some hint as to what he thought or felt?

"Of course," she choked out, because she realized he was awaiting her response. "You are right."

"There are too many eyes here," he said, and motioned his head toward the others. She followed where he indicated and found that, indeed, several members of the royal family and all the dignitaries were watching them.

"They are always on you, it seems," she said softly.

He nodded. "Yes."

"I cannot imagine the weight of that, Grantham." His mouth tightened and she stiffened. "Your Majesty," she corrected herself.

"I like when you call me by my name. Too much, perhaps." He shook his head. "This lot will likely take to their beds by midnight. Will you meet me in the library tonight?"

"Yes," she whispered.

"Very good. Excuse me."

Without another word or look her way, he stepped away. She stared after him, still as uncertain as she'd been before as to how their meeting would go. Would he cut her off? Punish her? Apologize?

Or did the fact that he'd told her he liked when she said his name mean that he would come to her and repeat what had happened before? She shivered at the thought, pleasure rippling through her almost against her will.

She glanced at the clock on the mantel. Midnight felt so very far away and she was certain she would be haunted by every tick of the clock until it came and they were together again. Alone again.

CHAPTER 11

Grantham had requested Ophelia meet him at midnight, but he hadn't been able to stay away long before that. He'd entered the library half an hour before and had been pacing the room ever since, jumping any time there was the slightest noise or movement in the hallway.

"You are king of a nation," he scolded himself, moving to the fire and stirring it gently with the iron. "You cannot be thwarted by one intriguing woman."

He said it and he wished he meant it, but as the door opened behind him and he pivoted to watch Ophelia enter the room, all thoughts of being strong faded. There was only her now and the very powerful desires he felt toward her.

She still wore her gown from supper, a honey-gold silk with a provocatively low neckline that was protected by just a swath of pale yellow lace. His mouth went dry at the sight of her and drier still when she reached behind her and closed the library door.

Her hands shook, revealing she was just as moved as he was, and she clasped them before her as she stood there by the door. Almost as if ready to run if need be.

"Good—good evening," she said, her voice cracking just a fraction.

Well, at least she was as nervous as he was. A great feat considering how confident she always seemed to be. There was something powerful about knowing he had chipped away at her in some of the same ways she always did to him. A triumph he ought not to celebrate and yet did.

"Please come in," he said.

She swallowed hard before she took one step forward. When he arched a brow, she huffed out her breath and took a few more to come closer. Not close enough by any means, but at least she was really in the room now.

Still, she said nothing, only continued to watch him, eyes wide. He shifted. This would fall on him, it seemed. As it should, considering their positions, he supposed.

"Obviously we must discuss what happened earlier this afternoon."

A flutter of a smile tilted the edges of her lips. "I can always depend on you to forgo small talk."

He angled his head. "Would you like me to ask about your evening first? Talk to you about the weather or the roads?"

He was pleased when the fire that was within her stoked back up in her eyes. She placed her hands on her hips and gave him that challenging smile that lit up the room like a candle. "Of course, Your Majesty. The weather has been wonderful this entire trip. I do love the end of the summer, the beginning of autumn. I imagine this island must blaze with color as the leaves turn."

He blinked. "Er, yes."

"As for the roads, I have not ventured from the palace overly much in the last few weeks, but given the fine weather, I would assume they are good. You would allow for no less, I think. And as for my evening..." She trailed off and now faltered, all the bravado wavering. "Well, it was fine. Except for being nervous about this meeting."

"You, *nervous*?" he asked with a low chuckle. "I shall never believe it, my lady."

She sighed. "And yet, it is true. Of course, with as much trouble as I give you, I know what you said a moment ago is also true. We must talk about what happened between us this afternoon."

And there it was. The game was over. The consequences begun. He rather regretted that. But he still took a deep breath. "I'm sorry I took advantage," he began.

Her eyes went wide. "Took advantage?" she repeated. "Of course you didn't. Perhaps I did."

He moved toward her, and now there was just a step between them. Not even a long step and she would be pressed close like she had been a few hours before. His body reacted immediately to that thought, all the blood rushing to exactly the wrong places. God's teeth, he had to focus.

"I could have stopped it if I had wanted to," he said, and his voice was only a touch strangled.

"And so could I," she argued. Then she pursed her lips. "Are you...are you sorry it happened? That you...that you touched me like that?"

He hesitated. For propriety's sake he supposed he should express regret at his actions, or at least at their location. And yet he couldn't. He didn't want to, because if he did, this would certainly be over. And maybe that was *right*, maybe that was *proper*...but it certainly wasn't good. It wouldn't feel good to cut this off without further discussion and exploration of what had happened, what it meant and what the future was because of it.

"No. I wanted you." He shut his eyes briefly, swallowed hard and then looked at her again. "I-I want you, Ophelia."

There was a moment when she swayed on her feet, her eyes grew wide as saucers. He had no idea if she was put off by that directness. Perhaps he had misread this entire exchange, every exchange with her. It was possible.

"I understand if you don't wish—" he began, but she cut him off when she stepped up, grasped his lapels to pull him down to her and kissed him.

She whimpered low in her throat as the kiss immediately deepened. He couldn't help it, after all, the moment they touched it was lightning and fire and chaos. He delved his tongue between her lips, tasting her like it had been years since he had the pleasure rather than hours. And she met him with the same desperation and drive that he brought.

But before it could go too far, she also pushed back, her breath short, her pupils dilated as she stared up at him. "I want you," she whispered. "I wanted what we did today. And I...I want more."

He licked his lips. There it was, not driven by him after all, but by this remarkable sprite of a woman who asked for what she desired. Took it if need be. And set him entirely on his head every time they got within fifty feet of each other.

He found himself smiling as he motioned to the chairs before the fire. "Sit," he ordered. "It seems we have a great deal to discuss."

He was ordering her to sit. There was a part of Ophelia that bristled at that, wanted to refuse just to tweak him. And yet she did as he asked. After all, the tweaking was all part of this game, wasn't it? She could see that now, perhaps she'd always seen it in some way. When she made him react to her, that was a flash of passion from him.

And she had just admitted that his passion was what she wanted most.

He took the place beside her, but sat at the front of the chair, leaned forward, entirely focused on her. When his dark gaze slid over her, she couldn't help but shiver in response. The desire she felt for him was outrageous, uncontrollable and overpowering.

She cleared her throat, trying to regain some purchase over

herself. "Your people consider sex differently, I think, yes? With quite a progressive mindset."

He nodded slowly and rubbed his palms on his trousers, drawing her attention to the thick, muscled thighs beneath. God's teeth, it wasn't fair for a man to be so perfectly formed.

"Er, yes, we do. Although we value responsibility and care, the concept that someone is damaged by an act that is entirely natural is not one we embrace. Most marriages do not begin with virgin participants of any sex, and dalliances are not looked on with a judgmental eye." He leaned a little closer. "But that is not true in England. There is a stigma in your Society to what we did today in the throne room. If you and I engaged in an affair that went even further, if I took your virginity, and then you went home…I would damage your future. That is not something I am willing to do, no matter how deep this desire goes."

She shifted. "An affair," she repeated, and was surprised that there were two reactions that moved through her. The first was a thrill. He wanted to go further than they had that day. To make love to her, to give her pleasure. And she wanted that just as much.

But the second reaction was just as powerful: disappointment. Why, she could not place. After all, she and Grantham were entirely different people on markedly different paths. She didn't want more than an affair, certainly. To be in his life forever? Of course she didn't want that.

"Obviously this is not something you have considered," he said when she was quiet too long. "I have overstepped."

She shook her head and reached for his hand. Their fingers tangled and he stared down at them, his breath catching. He was normally so stoic, so unreadable, that it gave her an uncommon thrill to move him. To make him show what he felt on every line of his handsome face. Right now it was that same desire that had started all this.

"It isn't that I haven't considered it," she corrected him.

"Grantham, I have pictured what that would be like probably more than I should."

"You have?" His voice broke and his gaze grew heated as he met hers.

She nodded. "I hesitated because I must disabuse you of a notion and I fear what your reaction will be. Forward-thinking or not."

His brow wrinkled. "What is it?"

"I am—" She let out her breath slowly and tried to meter her suddenly racing pulse. "I am not a virgin."

She held her breath as she awaited his reaction. She could have guessed down to every outrage what some men of her acquaintance would have said and done hearing this from her. And no matter what he said about Athawickian openness, that didn't mean he wouldn't see *her* differently.

But he sat steadily, his hand never leaving hers. He appeared interested, but not judgmental. Not even surprised, really. Although perhaps he wasn't. He might have guessed she wasn't entirely untested. Most virgins wouldn't have responded so enthusiastically to what he'd done earlier. There would have been more shock, she supposed.

"Do you want to tell me about it?" he asked softly.

She swallowed. "No," she admitted. "But I think I must. After all, we are talking about an affair, aren't we?"

"That doesn't mean you owe me any glimpse into your past. You've had a lover, which means I won't shock you as easily. You won't have pain if I take you. I'm glad to know so I can be more prepared. But you don't have to give me anything you don't want to share."

She drew back. That was entirely unexpected. This man was accustomed to knowing everything as king. To having his hand in all parts of his realm. That he would not push into her space, that he would not demand or cajole was remarkable.

Could she actually trust him? She hadn't trusted any man beyond her brother for years. But right now she felt like she could give that gift, one she treasured far more than she had ever treasured her maidenhead, to this man.

"It is a complicated story," she whispered. "One that not many know. Perhaps no one knows the whole of it. But I would like to tell you."

His expression gentled slightly. "I would like to hear it."

"At the very least it will give you something to lord over me when I tease you," she said, forcing a laugh because she needed this to be lighter, more playful.

He didn't allow it. He cupped her cheek with his unoccupied hand and stroked his thumb along the line of it. "I would never hold this against you. You may think many things of me, Ophelia. You might be right about them. But not that. Never that."

Her throat grew thick with that declaration and she dropped her gaze from his so he wouldn't see how much it meant. "His name was Erasmus Montgomery," she whispered. "His brother was best friends with mine, and so I had seen him here and there over the years. I had just turned twenty-one and I was so bloody bored of everything. All those seeking gentlemen who wanted a link to the Gilmore title or to attach themselves to my dowry. I was spending a few weeks in Bath, and suddenly Erasmus was there."

"By design?" Grantham asked softly.

She shrugged. "I suppose now I can see that it was. Back then I thought it providence. He was...fun to be around. Playful and untethered. He didn't seem interested in anything I could provide except for my good company. He rushed through a courtship and within weeks had asked me to marry him. I was foolish enough to say yes. It was all secret, of course, because we hadn't spoken to Gilmore. I said we had to do so and we agreed to meet in London a few days later."

She felt the heat in her cheeks, refused to look at Grantham as she fought for the words to continue. "Before we parted and he returned ahead of me, he asked me to allow him liberties. I was certain I could convince Nathan to approve the marriage, once he saw how happy I was with Erasmus. And if I couldn't, this would be a bargaining chip. So I...allowed it."

She moved to get up, to walk away. Grantham held her hand, only releasing her when she walked past him, pacing the room restlessly.

"Did you...like it?" he asked.

She froze. "Of all the questions I thought you would pose, that is not the one I expected."

He shrugged. "As I said, I do not judge the act. I am willing to wait out the story to understand. And I have a vested interest in your physical history. In what you have experienced and enjoyed... or not enjoyed."

"It was fine," she said. "I expected more, I suppose, since English society makes such a fuss over the act. But it was adequate. I was excited to know more, to find the paths to the pleasure that some spoke of when the act was described. But it was not to be."

"Why?" he asked.

She shook her head. "My brother had caught wind that I might have a suitor, that there might be something untoward about the situation, and he had been working diligently to uncover the truth. By the time I arrived in London, he had found out who I was with. And he was enraged."

Grantham stood. "But this man was brother to his friend. I would think the connection might please him."

"Perhaps it could have in a different life." She worried her hands before her. "But you see...oh, this is the part that will shock you. That might change how you see me."

Grantham took a long step toward her. "Never."

He believed that. She could feel it. But he didn't know. And it was better just to say the truth and let the consequences fill the room.

"Nathan had discovered that Erasmus was already married. In fact, he was a bigamist, with three poor wives who did not know the existence of each other."

Grantham's eyes went wide and he staggered back, the shock so clear on his face that she nearly laughed. At least she had moved him. Only she couldn't laugh because the memory was too sharp.

"I fear my expression when he told me was much the same as your own," she said softly. "I was horrified. Everything I had experienced and heard was a lie. All my future hopes and dreams were dashed."

"My God, Ophelia," Grantham said at last. "I cannot imagine how you felt. I'm so very sorry."

She blinked. "You—you don't judge me?"

"How could anyone? You were the victim of this bastard's schemes, as were his other wives. What happened?"

"Nathan sent me away immediately. I was just as happy to go, my humiliation was so complete. I went back to the country and tried to grieve the future that would never be. To understand how I had been such a fool."

"And what happened to this Montgomery fellow? I assume your brother called him out?"

"He was murdered shortly after my brother uncovered the truth," she whispered. "It was a scandal of all scandals years ago. The entire truth of his wives came out, though Nathan protected my name. There was an investigation into the murder. Nathan was even a suspect briefly, as were all the wives."

"Did they determine who did it?" Grantham asked.

She nodded. "Yet another woman who had been ensnared by him. The whole thing was covered up, as one does in Society. It's hardly ever spoken of now, except in the occasional whisper."

"What about the wives?" he asked.

She smiled, for their tales were public knowledge, so she was telling no secrets when she revealed their outcomes. "One married the investigator hired to solve the crime. One married Erasmus's brother."

Grantham's eyebrows lifted. "Truly?"

"They are deliriously happy with two children." She smiled as she thought of them. "As for the last, she…married my brother."

Grantham stared at her. "The Duchess of Gilmore?"

She nodded. "Abigail was the only legal wife and she accepted all of us so kindly when everything came out. We are all friends, a sisterhood created by one man's cruelty, his lies. Luckily there were happy outcomes for all involved. And I adore Abigail, as does my brother."

"That is a remarkable story," Grantham said slowly.

"It is," she agreed. "I was spared the social consequences thanks to my brother's protection. I repaid that by sparing *him* the whole truth. I told Priscilla that I surrendered my innocence to Montgomery, but no one else knows. Except you, I suppose."

She opened her mouth to say the rest but then closed it. There were some secrets no one knew. Even Priscilla. And he didn't need to know them either.

"You did nothing wrong," he said softly, bringing her back to him. "You were taken advantage of by a charlatan."

"And yet I will be seen as damaged if the truth comes out. As you said, our societies view this issue far differently." She sighed. "I will admit that it is why I have avoided marriage so studiously. I could never keep such a secret from someone I planned to marry, especially given the high value placed on virginity. I haven't met anyone who wouldn't count this fact against me. So I dance and I laugh and I refuse all proposals and interest."

"What do the duke and duchess say about that?"

She shrugged. "Luckily my brother has never been the kind of man who would force my hand. If I do not marry, I will become an eccentric spinster, I think. With money and independence." She forced a smile. "Not the worst fate."

"I suppose not," he agreed, and moved toward her. She shivered as he took her hand, drew her closer. "I am sorry you endured this, Ophelia."

For a moment the emotions she usually kept at bay when she

thought of her history washed over her. Overwhelmed her, and her eyes stung with tears. "I was a fool. And what happened changed me."

He nodded. "As would any affair *we* embarked on. I would not want to say otherwise and be just as unfeeling as Montgomery."

She frowned. "If you ever compare yourself to Erasmus Montgomery again, I shall call you out for pistols at dawn."

He laughed and the room seemed to lighten with the sound. "I would never think you would defend me so strenuously. You do not like me."

She pursed her lips. "I am endlessly frustrated by you, Your Majesty, as you are by me. But I would *never* compare you to that vicious, cruel bastard. And you are wrong that I would be changed by an affair we participated in. The circumstances are entirely different."

His brow knitted briefly, and she thought she saw a flash of regret in his eyes. But then it was gone. "I suppose we will both fully understand the limitations."

She nodded. "Exactly. And you would be careful, wouldn't you?" He tilted his head as if he didn't fully understand. She blushed. "A child. You would be careful not to create a child."

There must have been something in her tone that revealed her pure terror at that thought. His expression softened. "I would be very careful, Ophelia."

She sagged in relief. "Then my eyes are open, Grantham. I have no expectation of a future with you and know you do not desire that either. This would be an arrangement purely for pleasure." She hesitated. "Wouldn't it?"

She didn't know why she held her breath as she awaited his answer. Or why her heart sank the tiniest bit when he nodded.

"Yes." His voice was rough. "I would very much like to give you pleasure, Ophelia. So much pleasure."

"And I would like the same," she said with a smile, and edged a little closer to him.

She stared up into those dark eyes, the ones that dilated when she let her hand settle on his chest. She could feel the throbbing beat of his heart, the heat of him through his jacket. She wanted that heat so desperately. She wanted to forget all the rest, both the past and the future.

"Now," she murmured, then lifted on her tiptoes and kissed him again.

The entire room faded away as Ophelia traced the tip of her tongue over Grantham's lips. A soft entreaty, a quiet demand. One he couldn't deny, didn't want to deny anymore. This was happening, and now that the decision had been made, he surrendered himself fully to it and to her.

She wrapped her arms around his neck and lifted into him, the kiss deepening. God, she tasted like the headiest wine and he would be drunk on her and love every moment of it. Only he couldn't lose all his inhibitions. After the story she'd just told, he needed to be careful. Chivalrous.

She deserved that kind of tender care.

He tugged her closer, letting her body mold to his, and reveled in the soft, shaky sigh that she exhaled against his mouth. He could have kissed her for hours. In fact, he lost track of time as he did so, savoring every hitch of her breath, every sweep of their tongues. By the time he drew back to look into her eyes, he was panting, rock hard, and his hands shook with desire. She smiled up at him, wicked and knowing.

"I've never seen *that* look on your face before," she whispered, brushing her lips against his lightly.

"You'll see it a great deal from now on," he promised, and began to back her toward the settee. He pressed a hand into the small of her back and lowered her gently onto the cushions. She reached for him, but he dodged her and instead moved to the door.

"Are you leaving?" she asked, tone incredulous as she sat up on her elbows and tracked him.

"Not even if you offered me a million pounds sterling," he promised, and met her gaze over his shoulder as he turned the key in the lock.

"Ah, a very intelligent king," she teased.

"I can learn from the mistakes of others," he acknowledged. "Remi, especially, has been teaching me lessons for a very long time."

She choked out a laugh at his reference to the delicate position Remi and Priscilla had found themselves in just a week before. Of course, it had led to their marriage and that was what both of them wanted so…perhaps he had not been so much a fool after all.

Grantham pushed all that aside as he stripped out of his jacket and tossed it over the back of a chair without breaking his stride to her. She licked her lips, her blue eyes darkening with desire. "Take the rest off."

His eyebrows lifted. "I am not accustomed to being ordered about."

"I know," she said with a falsely solemn nod. "It's why I do it. To make your eye twitch like that."

"I would not put it past you," he grunted, but he did as she asked and unfastened his cufflinks, removed his vest and then unwound his cravat. She seemed mesmerized as she tracked the removal of every item.

At last, he unbuttoned his shirt, tugged it from his trouser waist and then pulled it over his head.

"Good God," she whispered, her gaze flitting over him. "That statue in the garden does you no justice."

He chuckled as he dropped to his knees beside the settee and leaned in to kiss her. "That statue," he said between kisses, "isn't even designed to look like my body. And it's missing a finger thanks to you."

"Thanks to *you*," she protested, pulling back from him with a bright smile.

"Thanks to us," he conceded. "Now I would very much like to remove some of your clothing if you'll allow it."

The smile faded and to his surprise her cheeks reddened.

"You don't want me to?" he asked gently.

She swallowed. "I do. All I have thought about since this afternoon was what it would feel like if your skin was on mine. How combustible that would be. How I would melt into you and forget which parts were mine and which were yours."

He shuddered at the description that somehow aroused him even further. His cock was almost painful now. "But?" he choked out.

"But it's been a while," she whispered. "And the idea of being naked with another person is still…a bit fraught."

He nodded. "I understand. If it helps, the last time I was naked with another person was also a good while ago."

She wrinkled her brow. "How long?"

He pondered the question. "Let's see…two years?"

Her eyes went wide. "Two years? You have not been with a lover for two years?"

"Would you like to declare it from the town square?" he asked.

She shook her head. "I'm sorry to be so boisterous, I'm simply surprised. After all, just…just look at you."

She punctuated the statement by stretching out a hand and touching his bare skin for the first time. Her fingers dragged along his collarbone and then lower, across one pectoral. It was fire, she was fire, he wanted to burn.

"I…" He cleared his throat and tried to do the same with his mind. "My father died just over a year ago and he was sick for many months before that. I had duties to attend to and could not be distracted." Truth be told, it was imperative he not be distracted now, either, but Ophelia was just too much to resist.

"I see." Her tone was softer. No longer teasing. She sat up, their faces even, noses almost touching. "Let's make it worth the wait for both of us."

He nodded and reached around to her back. He pulled her in for another kiss. Slow this time, deep. She relaxed against him and he unfastened her gown as he lost himself in her once again. He pulled it and her chemise forward, moving his lips to her neck and sucking gently. Only when he had reached her lower arms with the fabric did she pull away and, with a big breath, tugged her hands free.

She was naked from the waist up and she stared at him, watching him look at her. And look he did. She was glorious. Her breasts were small, with dark nipples that had puckered with the air and, he hoped, her growing arousal. He reached out, dragging his knuckles across one breast and smiling when she dipped her head back and shivered.

He couldn't resist the offer she made with that motion. He ducked his head and gently circled one nipple with his tongue.

"Oh God," she gasped, her hands coming up into his hair, holding him tighter against her.

He eased her back on the settee cushion once more and surrendered himself to her pleasure. He studied every reaction as he swirled his tongue around one nipple, then the other. As he sucked gently, then harder. He marked everything he did that made her grind up into him, that made her sigh or curse or grip his hair with both hands. Unlocking her pleasure was like magic and he never wanted to stop teasing and tormenting her just to hear her breath catch and her body tremble.

He hooked his fingers around the gown now tangled at her waist and tugged it. She broke the kiss and took another big breath before she lifted her hips and let him remove the beautiful layers of fabric and lace. Unlike earlier in the day, she wore no drawers, so all that was left were her stockings and slippers.

He stared down the length of her body, memorizing every curve with his eyes before he came to know them in great detail with his hands and his mouth and his tongue. He was truly going to enjoy this.

She leaned up and cupped his chin, forcing his gaze back to her face. "And now you need to remove the rest, or else it isn't fair."

He couldn't help but laugh, but nodded as he pushed from his knees and motioned her to scoot her legs over on the settee. When she'd allowed him a slender space, he perched on the edge and went to work on his boots. Once they were gone, he stood and arched a brow at her.

"Ready?"

She smiled. "You make it sound as if there should be trumpets sounding or—" Her words cut off as he shoved the trousers away and stood naked before her.

The King of Athawick was big. Ophelia had always been attracted to his solid, broad form, how tall he was. But now, staring at him naked, he felt *extremely* big. Bigger than Erasmus, who was her only frame of reference. She sat up fully and reached for him. Her hand shook as she closed it around his width and then traced his length in one stroke.

"Fuck," he grunted, his head tipping back.

A flutter worked through her at that curse. She'd never heard him swear before. He was always in too much control of himself to be vulgar. Which meant she had cracked that control and she loved it. Loved watching him shed the trappings of an institution and simply become a man.

Her man, at least for a while.

She edged closer and brushed her cheek against his cock, then darted her tongue against the head.

His eyes flew open and he stared down at her. "Ophelia."

She smiled at the plea in his tone. "Yes?" She licked him again.

"Don't play with fire," he ordered as he dropped back down to the settee, forcing her hand away and pressed his lips to hers.

His kiss was harder now, more driven, and she welcomed it. Because of her confession, she had felt him being cautious as he touched her. Careful, as if she were glass and he feared breaking her. What he didn't understand, what she couldn't say, was that she wanted to be broken. She wanted his passion, his drive, like she had felt as he licked her in the throne room. She wanted reckless abandon.

She dug her nails into his shoulders lightly, pulling him even closer, and he grunted against her mouth in a low, dangerous sound of pleasure.

"I want fire," she murmured against his mouth. "I want you."

He pulled away slightly and met her eyes. He was so close that it felt like there was only him in the world, or at least in her world. A feeling that was both terrifying and comforting.

He edged off the settee and back to his knees on the floor. Without saying a word, he cupped her hips and dragged her closer. Just as they had on the throne earlier that day, her legs fell open. Only this time she was naked. This time she knew what he could do with that tongue. He smiled, utterly wicked, as he massaged her outer lips, peeled them apart and then put his mouth on her for the second time that day.

She arched against him as he licked her, hard and fast. In a way, she supposed this was exactly what she'd demanded: fire. His mouth was fire against her, building a fire within her. She lifted to meet his strokes, hating and loving how easily he could take her to the edge. But once he got her there, he slowed down, never quite allowing her to fall.

It was torture, but the most wonderful kind. Pleasure was just there and he kept it out of reach, smiling against her as she writhed and tried to lift into him to take what he was withholding.

"Greedy, greedy," he murmured, sucking her clitoris lightly and then edging back when she cried out.

Before she could curse his name, he stroked two fingers across her entrance and then gently dipped the tips inside. She held her breath. Although she had touched herself since her time with Montgomery, she had never done that. Nothing had been inside of her since the one and only time Erasmus had taken her.

Until now.

Grantham slowed his tongue, circling her clitoris gently now as he slid inside to the first knuckles of his two fingers. He looked up at her, and she shivered at the image of this powerful man on his knees, asking her permission with his eyes as he pleasured her.

With Erasmus, his taking had hurt. He certainly had not paid so much attention to her body before he just…slammed inside of her and changed her forever.

Grantham was different. In every way. She was so slick with need, so close to the edge of pleasure, that his fingers only made her feel full, stretching her, yes, but not damaging or hurting. She clenched around him, testing what it would feel like, and he sucked her clitoris harder before he grunted like he liked what she was doing.

"You want it?" he asked, looking up at her again. "Take it then."

Without another word, he slid his fingers farther into her, gently flexing them inside as he began to suck her clitoris with far more focus. She did as he had ordered, lifting against him, grinding for release, worrying about nothing but her own pleasure.

When it hit, it was more powerful than anything she'd ever felt before. A crash of sensation that felt like it took over her entire body, erasing all fear and worry, all pain of memory. There was only pleasure and it went on and on as she trembled against his mouth and his curling fingers.

He gave her no respite, licking her as she spasmed until she went weak against the settee, her gasps and cries fading.

Only then did he rise over her, aligning his big body to hers, stroking the entrance to her sex with the head of his cock. She leaned up on her elbows and watched as he gently worked himself inside of her.

The stretch of his fingers had been nothing in comparison, and yet there was nothing unpleasant about what he did. Her sensitive body sang as he filled her inch by inch, slowly until he was fully seated and he shuddered.

She flexed again and his face contorted with pleasure. "Christ, Ophelia," he grunted, and then thrust gently.

She gasped at the slide of him inside of her and the echoing sensations of pleasure that immediately were reborn in every nerve ending in her body. How was that possible? How could he make her feel so good, over and over, like a craving that she could fulfill at will?

They moved together, slowly at first, learning each other's bodies, finding the rhythm that best pleased them both. But as that pleasure mounted, his intensity increased in equal measure. His thrusts grew faster, he cupped the back of her neck and their foreheads touched, breath mingling as they both panted in need and pleasure and surrender.

His hips ground against hers and she lifted to meet him, shocked when another orgasm hit her like wildfire. It seemed that was what he was waiting for. He held her gaze, taking harder and faster, dragging her through pleasure, working for his own.

She could see the end was near from the growing wildness of both his expression and his thrusts. She tensed a little, hoping he remembered his promise to be careful. It seemed he did, because at last he withdrew from her with a roar and stroked his cock, pumping into his hand before he pressed his mouth to hers, heated and then gentler, slower.

She pulled him to cover her, sighing at the feel of his weight pushing her into the cushions. She was…light. Unburdened, as if these powerful moments had given her freedom. It had definitely not been like that with Erasmus. Odd that the same act could feel so different.

Grantham lifted his head and looked down at her. For the briefest of moments, she saw so much in his eyes. Down to the depths of his soul in a way she'd never felt before. But as if he sensed that too, he turned his face, blocked her from the heart of him and carefully got up.

She frowned as she watched him grab for his trousers and cover himself. When he had done so, he glanced back at her. "I didn't hurt you?"

"I think you know you didn't," she said softly. "You were very careful not to."

He shrugged. "At the end not as much. It was a bit…animal at the end."

"I liked it," she reassured him. "All of it."

The hint of a smile tilted his lips, but he didn't allow it to fully bloom. The king was returning, that was clear. The man packed away, at least for a while.

"And do you wish to…to continue this arrangement?" he asked.

She laughed despite herself. "So formal, Your Majesty. Would you like to extend the invitation in writing?"

His brow furrowed at the teasing, at how easily they fell back into the roles that had created such tension between them. Now she could see how much they were part of building toward these heated moments. Truly a game. She danced around him, pushing him closer and closer to an edge until he could no longer fight her and he cracked. And then? Well, he unleashed that animal side he had spoken of a moment before.

And she could not wait to replay that scenario all over again.

"Would that be wise?" he asked, but she felt the edge to his voice. The hunger that had been there from the start but she'd never understood.

"Perhaps not," she conceded. "But if you're asking me if I'd like to be bedded by you again…yes, Your Majesty. I would definitely welcome an invitation to this dance."

His expression softened and now he did smile, albeit briefly. "Good." He cleared his throat. "Tomorrow night? My chamber."

She almost laughed. He was *scheduling* their assignation. Which was so perfectly him that she couldn't help but be warmed by it. "Yes."

He shifted and then picked up her gown and chemise, tangled together at his feet. "May I help you dress?"

She got up, tracking how he watched her as she moved toward him. She ignored the dress he extended to her and instead stepped into his chest, letting her body brush his, and she leaned in to kiss his cheek, the corner of his mouth, then his mouth fully. He grumbled against her, his arms coming around her to pull her closer.

She drew back with a smile. "Thank you, Grantham," she whispered.

His brow wrinkled. "For what?"

"For all of this," she said.

He considered her a moment and then stepped away, detangling her gown and underthings. "Your chemise, my lady," he said, handing it over.

She laughed as she tugged it over her head, but there was a niggling sense in the back of her mind. A sensation that although she had gained something tonight, that they had also missed out on an opportunity for something more.

And that more was one thing neither of them would be able to give.

CHAPTER 13

If Grantham had convinced himself, as he tossed and turned in his bed, that finally giving over to the desire he felt for Ophelia would make him more able to concentrate, the next morning proved him entirely wrong. He sat at the head of the breakfast table, his mother at the opposite end, the counts and remaining council members on either side of them, and he could not attend fully. No, his errant mind kept going back to thoughts of Ophelia arching beneath him. Ophelia's tongue swiping across the head of his cock. Ophelia's orgasm milking his own.

"But that is not the point, is it, Your Majesty?"

Grantham jolted back to the present and looked at the man who had spoken. Count Hadley of the eastern part of the island, who, unlike Count Friskar, was *not* a friend. Hadley had been over-reaching for decades. Even Grantham's father had been irritated by it.

"Then what *is* the point, Hadley?" Grantham asked as mildly as he could manage when his mind was spinning so restlessly.

"Uprising is not good for anyone," he snapped. "And how you can stand by so calmly when it is almost at your doorstep is beyond my reasoning. Do you not care for your country? For those of your class? An overreaching populous must be crushed or we risk losing control, like the English did in America not that long ago. Is that what you want, Your Majesty?" He wrinkled his brow. "A...democracy?"

Grantham swallowed. He had studied in England for a year and the rebellion of the colonies had been covered, with their unique spin on the topic, of course. It had been a fascination to him, the idea of a people governing themselves. Upon his return, he had even tried to broach the idea with his father.

And the punishment for such thoughts had been swift and cruel. "I want what is best for the people. That is supposed to be who I serve," he said softly.

There was a flicker in Hadley's eyes at that response and his gaze slipped, just briefly, to Blairford, who Grantham knew was stationed behind him, taking notes on this unofficial meeting. Now why had he looked at the courtier? Grantham's unease elevated.

He might have addressed it, or at least tried to suss out the truth in a more subtle way, but before he could, Ophelia appeared in the breakfast room door. She came to a halt, her face darkening pink as she looked first at him and then at the others gathered there.

"Oh, I beg your pardon," she said. "I was told there was a gathering here to join, but I did not realize it was some kind of official business."

The gentlemen all hurried to rise and Grantham joined them. It was odd that this explosive storm of a woman brought peace into the room when she entered. Just the tiniest edge of it, but there it was. For the first time since she'd left his side last night he felt...calm.

"Oh, please do join us," Queen Giabella said. "We should enjoy a friendly breakfast before our guests depart."

There was no doubting the firm resolve of his mother's tone, and Grantham smothered a smile. She had been putting cranky dignitaries in their places for decades, since before he was born, likely before she even married his father. It came so naturally to her and no one dared deny her.

Instead, the gentlemen all became more relaxed at her order. No longer adversarial, which at least was something. Even Hadley shifted his attention. Only he shifted it to Ophelia, which wasn't entirely pleasant. He looked at her like she was something he could pluck.

"Why don't you sit beside me, Lady Ophelia?" the older man asked, motioning to the empty chair that had meant to be taken by one of the leaders who had been called away on an emergency before breakfast.

Ophelia inclined her head. "Oh, you are all too kind. I am sorry I interrupted, but I am pleased to be welcomed so warmly."

She took her place beside Hadley and the gentlemen all retook their seats as one of the footmen ran off to get a plate for Ophelia. As they waited, she glanced again down the long table at Grantham. She smiled slightly, but it was warm, and once again he felt another level of tension leave his body.

"You mustn't apologize," Hadley was saying. "After all, we were just talking of serious matters. Nothing that you should trouble yourself with. And nothing that will change, I fear."

Hadley shot him a look and the tension returned immediately. The troublemaking bastard was going to be an issue Grantham would have to add to the pile pressing weight to his back.

"I have found that everything changes in the end," Ophelia said in that cheerful tone that seemed to brighten everything around her, even when she was making a point or bringing someone down a peg. "That is the nature of the world, is it not?"

Hadley pursed his lips and leaned back in his chair a fraction to look at her with disdain. Of course he did. To a man like Hadley, a woman like Ophelia was merely dressing for his arm. He had no respect for her. And if she dared to go against him, as she just had, he would attempt to put her in his place.

"I wonder how much you truly understand Athawickian politics, my lady?" he said, and scorn dripped from every word.

Grantham fisted a hand on the table, ready to push to his feet and call the man out for being rude to a guest of the royal family. But Ophelia glanced his way again and this time arched a brow. A silent order for him to be still. Not interfere.

"I think I would be a fool to think that I knew the nuances of a county's political situation that is not my own, no matter how much I read about the subject or asked questions of people who do know," she began. "Even those who live in a place all their lives can be *ignorant* and closed-minded to all the facts, can't they?"

Hadley opened his mouth as if to speak, but she didn't allow it and carried on. "But I will say that I have observed your king both in London and here since my arrival, and I can see that he and his family truly do care about their country. About its people."

Hadley's lips pursed. "Its people."

"What is a nation if not its people? The humblest of them make up the entire backbone of a place. They sail your ships and make your goods, they plow your fields and serve your supper. They create all the wealth and yet benefit only a fraction from it. Ignore them and crush them at your own peril, Count Hadley."

There were a few smiles amongst the others as well as some serious expressions, as if what she'd said sank in a fraction. Grantham watched in amazement at how easily she could captivate a room, turn its inhabitants in her direction without having to shout or bang her hand on a table.

She truly was a marvel.

"It seems you have been talking to our king," Hadley said after a pause.

"How so?" she asked, smiling up at the footman who placed a plate before her.

"You and he are in accord about this matter, it seems," Hadley said. "I suppose time will tell if you...and he...are correct."

"That is always the way of the world," Ophelia laughed. "Now, I must ask you, my lord…I have heard that your part of the island, the eastern part, is home of a most unusual fox, is that true?"

Hadley's nostrils flared at the change of subject, but the man had been in politics long enough to know when he had been beaten. He shifted and forced a smile. "Indeed it is, my lady."

He proceeded to talk to her about the silver fox that was often seen in the woods in his portion of the island. Which led to discussion of the other fine and rare things that were to be found in all the corners of this place Grantham loved so deeply. He watched as the dignitaries lit up as Ophelia asked them about their people and land. And in the end, all the tension was gone. Even Hadley was smiling when the plates were cleared away and the time had come for the official departures.

Ophelia joined the family at the front stair, waving goodbye to the carriages and horses as they rode away. Queen Giabella smiled at Ophelia.

"You handled them with great aplomb, my lady," the queen said. "As one who was once a stranger to this land, who also had to manage men with little thought to my assets beyond the physical, it was something to see."

Ophelia bent her head at the praise. "Thank you, Your Majesty. If I am compared to you in any way, that is the deepest compliment."

Giabella shot Grantham a look and then went back inside, which left him alone with Ophelia on the stair. He reached for her at last, touching just her hand and wishing he could do more. "Good morning," he said.

She smiled. "Good morning to you, or what is left of it." Her smile faltered. "I can see how much their presence weighs on you, what they want and drive for."

He shrugged. "It isn't something to concern yourself with."

Her expression hardened and she slid her hand from his. "I suppose not. I wish I could stay and talk more, but I promised Priscilla I would walk with her in the garden this morning, so I should go see if she has managed to rouse herself from their tower."

He inclined his head. "I have things to do, as well."

She started to go, but he caught her hand again, keeping her in place. She stared up at him, blue eyes wide and filled with desire and peace and passion.

"What is it?" she asked gently.

He drew in a shaky breath. "As much as I enjoyed having you at my table this morning, I recall you saying someone directed you to join what was meant to be a private political gathering. Who was it?"

She shook her head. "I fear I don't know his name. But it was one of your courtiers. Tall man, blond hair. I knew I interrupted the moment I came into the room, so I do apologize again."

He lifted his hand, tracing her cheek briefly. "No apology needed. You were a very welcome addition. Next time I would invite you myself."

Her cheeks flushed and there was no mistaking the pleasure in her gaze even as she stepped away. "I hope to see you later, Your Majesty."

"And you," he said. She slipped into the palace and he stood on the steps alone for a moment, looking out at the carriages exiting the gate in the distance.

How he wished he could stay in the pleasant world that Ophelia created with her mere presence. To pretend he was just a man enthralled with a fascinating woman. But he wasn't. And he had something to address.

Now.

He strode back into the house and found Blairford already waiting in the foyer, scratching notes on a paper. Grantham stopped and stared, taking in the man who had helped run this household, this country, this family, for most of his life.

"I need to speak to you in my study," he said, motioning Blairford to follow as he paced past him.

The courtier did as he had been told, following him wordlessly. When they entered the study, Blairford closed the door behind himself and stood at the ready, watching Grantham carefully. "What can I do, Your Majesty?" he asked at last.

Grantham put his hands behind his back, widened his stance. "I found it interesting that Count Hadley was using almost the exact language today as you do to discuss the problem with the uprising."

There was not even a flicker of concern across Blairford's expression as he shook his head. "I think it is a common concern amongst the leaders of this country. If we all repeat the same sentiment—"

"Stop." Grantham held up a hand. "Blairford, you have served this country and this family for many years. And I do not wish to be reductive when it comes to your role and how appreciated it has been. But *you* are not a leader of this country."

Now there *was* a reaction. Brief but powerful hatred washed across every feature of the man before him. Then it was gone. Only Grantham had seen it, had felt it. And this time he couldn't ignore it anymore.

"You were the one who called Priscilla's parents here, weren't you?" he asked.

Blairford shifted. "I think we have discussed this, sir—"

Grantham took a step closer. "You wrote the letter that inspired them to sail to Athawick. And once they had arrived, you sent them to her room purposefully, in order to sow chaos and discontent between my brother and me. In order to keep me from turning to anyone but you for counsel."

"I assure you that isn't true, Your Majesty." The courtier was shaking his head now, his gaze darting about as if he were trying to find some answer, some exit that would appease Grantham.

Only now there was none.

"How many times have you gone behind my back since I took this crown?" Grantham asked softly. "How many times have you spoken out of turn in order to steer the agenda of this institution in the direction you have decided was best? Is that why you had one of your lackeys send Ophelia into the breakfast room this morning? More disruption?"

Blairford's jaw had tightened with every question. "Protecting your interests and what you father and all the kings before him built is my duty, Your Majesty."

Grantham heard the disdain in the title. Had it always been there? Had he just ignored it because he saw no other way forward?

"My father is no longer on the throne," he said softly.

There was a moment's hesitation and then Blairford smiled, but it was as cold as one of the sharks that stalked the boats in the sea. Empty and predatory, a mask. "*That* is most definitely true."

Grantham gripped his hands into fists at his sides. "I would like to thank you for your service, Blairford. And you will be rewarded for it with a fine pension and a lovely home either here or elsewhere if you would prefer it. But your services are no longer required."

Blairford's mouth dropped open and the papers in his hands slipped to the floor. "You cannot mean that."

"And yet I do," Grantham said. "There has been a shift in power with the death of the previous king. I should have realized that we had differing views that cannot be aligned. That it is time to offer your position to someone new. Someone who better understands the direction in which *I* would like to steer this country."

Now there was no concealing the hatred that Blairford felt for him. His face turned almost purple as he shook his head. "As if you could steer anything on your own. You are a weak, shiftless fool and without me you will watch this country fall. You will be remembered as the king who lost everything and I will laugh from the sidelines."

Grantham flinched. After all, those were his greatest fears: that he would fail his country and his people. But he pushed it aside and motioned for the door. "We are finished."

Blairford didn't move, and as Grantham went to open the door and make his position clearer, the courtier reached out and grabbed his lapel, yanking him closer.

For what felt like forever they stood that way, faces close, and then Grantham pressed both hands to Blairford's chest and shoved. As Blairford stumbled back, it was like he woke up and realized what he'd done. The color drained from his cheeks.

"You know exactly what the punishment for such a thing would have been in the past, so be happy that I am not my father." Grantham stepped to the door and called out, "Guard?"

One of the finely liveried soldiers who served as sentry in the halls rushed forward. "Yes, Your Majesty?"

"Mr. Blairford is to be escorted from the palace grounds immediately. He is not welcome back and all the guards should know this, though I will express it personally to the captain shortly." The guard's eyes went wide but he did not interrupt, simply caught Blairford by the arm. "That will be all."

Grantham didn't look at Blairford again as he was all but dragged down the hallway, muttering his grievances loudly with every step. But when he entered his study, Grantham's hands began to shake.

He reached for the bell and stopped. Normally it would be the man he'd just tossed onto his backside would be the one who came when he rang. So he ignored the bell and instead stepped back into the hallway. He found a maid who had been dusting in the closest parlor. She jumped when he said, "Excuse me?"

"Y-Your Majesty," she gasped, raising her duster to her chest. "H-how can I help?"

"I need the queen," he said. "And Dashiell Talbot with her. And my brother." He frowned. "And the Earl of Bramwell and my sister, as well. Can you find someone to fetch them all and have them come to my study immediately?"

She looked confused. Soon she wouldn't be. Soon the firing of the most senior member of palace staff would spread like wildfire through the estate and then the kingdom. He shuddered to think what would be said. The fact that this institution was in chaos had to be becoming clearer with each day. "I-I will, sir. Straight away."

He returned to the study and sat down at his desk. He'd spent years under his father's thumb and continuing to work with Blairford had been a part of that.

Now he was free. And it was terrifying and liberating all at once. It took a short while, ten minutes at most, though it felt like ten hours, but bit by bit his family joined him. And when any of them saw his face, they looked…sick. As if they already knew he was failing. As if they were waiting for more of it.

He steadied himself as Remi joined them last and shut the door. "You look like hell," his brother said.

Grantham sighed. "I just dismissed Stephen Blairford from service to the Crown."

For a moment the room was nothing but stunned silence as they all stared at him. Then Remi barked out a laugh and crossed the room to slap his upper arm. "Good work, Your Majesty."

"Hateful man," Sasha agreed, clutching Thomas's arm all the harder. "He was a wretched thing and I am glad to see the palace rid of him."

Grantham shifted his attention to his mother and Dashiell. Giabella looked stunned, truly stunned. Dashiell was, as he always was in these matters of state, unreadable.

"Mama," Grantham said softly. "Your opinion on this matter is the most important to me. What do you think?"

"I think that Stephen Blairford overstepped in his duties for decades. I once counseled your father to make a similar decision with…" Her mouth twisted. "…unpleasant results."

Dash did stand a little taller at that statement. Grantham smiled. The secretary had always been her champion. He appreciated that.

"I don't know the man as well as the rest of you," Sasha's husband Thomas, the Earl of Bramwell, said. "Except from the tales told by my wife. What did he do today that inspired this action?"

Grantham sighed and told the story, including the part where Blairford had dared to grab him. When it was over, he sighed. "Of course this is not going to strengthen my position, the position of the Crown, with everything else going on. And I have no idea what Blairford will do outside of these walls."

"I wouldn't put it past him to do anything to hurt you," Sasha said.

Grantham looked at her, his sweet adoptive sister. "Father should have sacked him years ago for how he treated you. I'm sorry I waited so long to do the same."

She shook her head and smiled. "You are not and never will be to blame for anything your father did or didn't do to protect me, Grantham. And I adore you."

He smiled at the show of support.

"What do you need?" Remi asked.

Grantham stiffened. Since his father's death over a year ago…no, even before that…he had bristled at the idea that he needed help, even from his family. King Alistair had told him over and over that he was too weak to be king, and that voice always rang in his head when he felt the desire to ask for assistance.

Even today it echoed, and he hesitated even though this was exactly why he'd called them to his side.

Remi took his arm again, this time gently, and Grantham saw everything he adored in the brother who was so opposite from himself. He'd tried to push Remi away for so long, another symptom of the cruelty their father had poured down over them all for so many years.

But now he covered Remi's hand with his own and nodded. "I…I do need help," he said softly. He turned toward his mother and Dash again. "Dash, I trust you more than anyone else who works in this household."

Dash blinked, his pride in that fact clear on his face. "Thank you. How can I help? I will do anything you need."

"Will you find me a new head courtier?" Grantham asked. "I would ask you—" At that Giabella grew pale and her gaze darted to Dash. "—but I do not think my mother could spare you." When he added the last, he saw the queen sag with relief.

And he realized, his mind spinning, how much she cared for Dash. *Cared* for him, not as a friend, not as a trusted employee, but as something far more. And by the way Dash looked back at her, comforting her with just a quick look, that feeling might be returned.

Why had Grantham never recognized that before? That bond between them? Why could he see it now? Nothing had changed except…

Except for Ophelia.

He pushed that thought away as Dash nodded. "Of course I will do so. I have a few thoughts on that matter already. And I will help the new staff weed out any others who are more loyal to Blairford than they are the Crown. Shall I start straight away before the rumors of what happened with Blairford spread too widely?"

"Please," Grantham said.

"Thank you, Dash," Giabella said, touching the secretary's hand before he darted from the room. Grantham looked at her a fraction of a moment more, still stunned that he had finally realized this about his mother's internal life. But that was a subject for another day.

"I think that is the best I can hope anyone can do for me," he said. "I just wanted you all to hear what had happened from my lips."

"God's teeth, Grantham," Sasha shocked him by snapping as she released Thomas and came to him. "Stop this now—you are going to allow the rest of us to help you."

Remi nodded. "Well said, Sasha. You've locked us out of your problems long enough. We are a family, damn it. And we're going to help you. Now tell us what you need."

Grantham bent his head and the words he had held back seemed to press into him, pressure on a dam that could not hold. When he finally began to speak, the relief was massive.

"The…the situation with the rebellion is not getting better," he said softly. "In fact, that is why I sent Ilaria and Jonah to the southern realm. They're trying to find a leader for the group who I can meet with."

Remi's expression softened and he slung an arm around Grantham's shoulders. "What else?"

The words continued to spill. All of Grantham's fears, all of his worries and failings. And they heard them all and slowly began to offer support, assistance. Love. Love that had been discouraged by the previous king, but that he saw now had always been present.

And now he wasn't alone in trying to solve this problem. He had them. And he had Ophelia. Although she was a temporary balm. He couldn't come to depend on her too powerfully, because in the end she wouldn't be here.

They had both made that clear. And he couldn't forget it.

CHAPTER 14

Ophelia clung to Priscilla's arm, turning her face toward the warmth of the sun as they strolled through the garden together. It had been a wonderful hour together, and she realized how much she missed this private time with her dearest friend.

"Goodness, whatever shall I do once I'm back in London all alone, without you to walk with?"

Priscilla tightened her grip on Ophelia and shivered. "That is the only thought that intrudes upon my otherwise perfect happiness. You are my dearest friend and I have a hard time imagining a life where I cannot simply run to you to talk about serious things or silly things, happy and sad things."

"We'll write," Ophelia promised her.

"And visit," Priscilla offered. "You will come here all the time, probably on the royal ship every time Ilaria and Sasha come home. I will insist on it."

Ophelia smiled at the pretty picture that presented. And yet in her heart, she ached. She and Grantham would end this thing between them when she left Athawick in what felt like such a short time now. Would he want her to return and remind him of his lapse in judgment? When he married, would he wish to have her haunting the corners of his home, right in front of his queen?

Would she be able to bear seeing him with some other woman?

"You are suddenly silent," Priscilla said softly. "Would you like to talk about it?"

"Talk about what?" Ophelia asked with a shake of her head. "There is nothing to talk about."

"In the same way there was nothing to talk about when I was sneaking around with Remi?" Priscilla asked gently. When Ophelia couldn't bring herself to answer, her friend smiled. "You know I am a princess now."

Ophelia joined her in smiling. "Yes, you far outrank me, Your Highness." She gave a playful curtsey.

"I do. And so I demand that you share what is going on with you. You and Grantham."

Ophelia stopped walking. She all but stopped breathing at that order. She pivoted to face Priscilla, opening and shutting her mouth as she tried to find an explanation for what her friend had apparently already seen. Priscilla's expression remained gentle as she did so, kind, because she could be nothing but kind.

"I-I was going to tell you," Ophelia said at last. "I didn't know how."

"Why not?" Priscilla asked, still gentle. "After all, Remi and I were not so different."

"Oh, but you are," Ophelia said. "You and Remi love each other, and Grantham and I...don't." Why was it so hard to say that? She shook her head. "What we are engaged in is truly an affair and nothing more."

"That is a very familiar tune you are playing," Priscilla said with a laugh. "It is the same thing I told myself, after all, when Remi first... touched me. I thought I could hold my heart separate from my body. I promised myself that I would. And here I am, married to him." There was a dreamy joy to her face, and then her eyes lit up.

"Ophelia, we shall be sisters! In truth…well, in marriage, anyway. And you won't have to leave, so we will be together!"

Ophelia's head had begun to spin at the utter certainty her friend had about her future. It was one she smashed down any time it reared its silly head. But now Priscilla spun tales and it was hard not to picture being here forever. Being Grantham's forever.

She blinked those thoughts away. "You are ahead of yourself by leagues, my love," she insisted. "This is not the same. Grantham and I are entirely different people."

"As if Remi and I aren't," Priscilla said with a laugh. "A wallflower and a rake, how different could you get?"

"But Grantham has responsibilities that no one else in his family does," Ophelia insisted. "He is not looking for a queen, especially while all this unrest remains around him." Priscilla opened her mouth to speak, but Ophelia continued without allowing it. "And even if he were, all his siblings have chosen English spouses. Certainly Grantham would need a political alliance with someone from his own country." She blinked at the truth of that. "Or another ally to build his strength of position."

"But…but that would only be a political match," Priscilla said. "A miserable thing. You cannot want that for him."

Ophelia shrugged and it did nothing to lessen the sting of what she was saying. The truth of it sinking into her every pore and vein, burning like fire. "Sometimes that is the sacrifice one must make for a country," she whispered. "So yes, Grantham and I are…we are sharing in something wonderful."

"Oh, Ophelia." Priscilla took her hand.

Ophelia smiled and wished that her eyes didn't sting with tears. "It *is* wonderful. So much better than anything I've ever experienced. And that is a gift he has given me that I will not soon forget. The gift I give in return is pleasure, a little break from the pressure on his shoulders. And the fact that I shall never ask for more than he can give."

As she said it, she realized that was a promise she was making to herself. To him, without him even being present.

"I suppose I do understand," Priscilla said. "Remi worries so about him, if this eases Grantham's soul then it is a wonderful thing. Even if I did wish for more for both of you."

Ophelia shifted. "Yes, Remi. You won't tell him, will you?"

Priscilla's gaze slid away, the answer to the question even before she spoke. "I could tell you no, but…but we don't keep secrets from each other. If he asks, I can't lie. At any rate, I can tell you that he suspects something between you already. He has for weeks, even before we were together."

"What?" Ophelia burst out. "Why in the world would he suspect something?"

"Because he's clever," Priscilla offered. "And he has eyes in his head, Ophelia. The moment you and Grantham are in a room together, there is a spark. Perhaps you both tried to make it adversarial, but it's evident there is powerful attraction. And I'm glad you get to have…fun, at least. You deserve pleasure. So does he."

Ophelia sighed and took Priscilla's arm again as they started back toward the palace once more. Although she felt a certain sense of relief that at last her friend knew about what was happening, she was still unsatisfied with the conversation. It had only laid bare facts she hadn't wanted to face. Both about the origins of her relationship with Grantham and the reasons why it could never be more than what it was.

They walked up the stairs to the terrace and back into the house through one of the parlors. Priscilla was kind enough to change the subject as they went, and they were laughing about a mutual acquaintance in London when they entered the hallway. Laughter that ended as Remi came racing up the hallway, the most serious expression on his face that Ophelia had ever seen.

He rushed past them and then stopped, pivoted back and leaned down to kiss Priscilla. "Good morning, you."

"What is going on?" Priscilla asked, even as her cheeks flamed from his very public ardor. "You look concerned."

He smiled at Ophelia as if he hadn't quite noticed her with Priscilla there. "I fear you are a guest of a household in uproar, Ophelia. And it shall only be worse. Grantham has sacked Blairford."

Ophelia gasped. "What? His head courtier?"

"Indeed." Remi's lips pursed. "That bastard was always hated by all the siblings, but it seems he was stirring pots behind the scenes even more than we suspected."

Ophelia glanced down the hallway toward Grantham's study. "Is the king…is he well?"

Remi exchanged a quick glance with Priscilla that was impossible to ignore, and now it was Ophelia who blushed. God's teeth, she really was obvious. A strange thing—she'd always been able to keep her secrets before. But with Grantham it seemed she wore them out in public.

To her detriment, perhaps.

"He is…" Remi shook his head. "I admit, I've never seen him so shaken. Actually, I'm pleased I found you two. Priscilla, will you come with me? We are going to announce the marriage tomorrow, and I need your input and help with some arrangements."

Priscilla's eyes went wide. "I-I thought we were postponing that for a while, to allow things to calm down a bit after all the other changes."

He shook his head. "Blairford may cause more trouble and this story will spread far and wide. The family decided to control the narrative with our story instead."

"A distraction," Priscilla breathed. "Of course." She turned toward Ophelia. "I hate to cut our time short—"

Ophelia waved her off. "This is important. Go!"

Priscilla caught Remi's hand and they raced off together, leaving Ophelia alone in the hallway. She knew what she ought to do: go upstairs and keep out of everyone's way. She had no part in this development. She was not family, she was barely a friend to these people. Their time together had been so short.

And yet that wasn't what she did. Instead, she began to move toward Grantham's study. A foolhardy decision, of course. Every time she pressed him or offered her help, he pushed her away. Today would likely be no different. She might even make things worse.

And yet she needed to see him. To show him that she was there, even if he didn't want her there. To offer him support that was only for him, because this *wasn't* her country or her family.

She reached the huge carved door and stood there. It was cracked a fraction and she couldn't hear voices. If he was inside, it didn't sound like anyone else was with him at the moment.

She extended a shaking hand and pushed open the door, uncertain what reception she would receive from the man within, but still needing to see him, to be with him. She just couldn't analyze why too deeply or else risk a broken heart.

~

Grantham stood at the window to his office, staring out. He could see the tall spires on some of the buildings at the town below and the sea even farther past. His home.

And he was destroying it, he feared. Tearing it apart with bad decisions just as his father had claimed he would over and over since Grantham was just a boy.

The door behind him shut and he pivoted to see who had entered. He expected a family member or Dash, but instead it was Ophelia who stood there hovering by the door. A ray of sunshine just out of his reach, but oh so warm and welcoming even from a distance.

"Grantham," she said softly.

He could see she knew what had happened. Remi, he would guess, was the culprit for that revelation. Not that it mattered, because soon everyone would know. And it was good that he didn't have to tell her. He wasn't up to repeating the story.

She stepped closer, her expression softening with understanding and warmth and…and pity. She pitied him, he feared. Worse, he feared he was pitiable. But he didn't want that from her, not from anyone. His pride could not abide it.

So instead of letting her speak or comfort or commiserate, he crossed to her in a few long strides, pressed her back against the door behind her and dropped his mouth to hers. She hesitated in response for a moment, as if she was confused by his sudden passion, but then she shifted. Her body softened against his, her arms wound up around his neck, her mouth opened for him as she sighed against his lips.

That response changed his own. He slowed, actually savoring this moment, letting pleasure wash away some of his regret, some of his anxiety about everything he'd done wrong and would do wrong in the future. He could forget all that when he touched her. Perhaps that was foolish or ill-advised—certainly it was fleeting—but he would take it. And take her.

He needed to take her.

He pulled away from the kiss and slowly reached behind her, turning the key to lock them in. She held his gaze as he did so, nodding to answer the question he hadn't asked. He all but sagged with her consent and leaned a hand on either side of her against the door, caging her in as she lifted for yet another searing kiss.

After what felt like the most blissful eternity, they shifted, moving together as if they shared a mind, a body. He guided her back toward the settee before his fire. Honestly, at some point he needed to do this with her on a bed rather than a couch, but that was for later.

Right now he sank down and couldn't help but let out a quiet sigh. She sat beside him but arched a brow instead of returning to those wonderfully drugging kisses.

"Grantham," she whispered, and there was reality, coming back to the edges of his mind.

He shook his head as he reached out to cover her hand. "I have talked about it ad nauseam, Ophelia. I cannot say the words one more time."

He expected her to spar with him, as she was so driven to do. Perhaps she would even mean it to be playful, but today he was not up for it. Still, he braced for the game.

Only it never came. Instead her expression softened. She reached up and traced his cheek with her palm, then lower, down his shoulder, his chest, his stomach. He let his eyes flutter shut and simply sank into the pleasure of that touch. When her fingers danced over his body, even through all the layers of clothing that separated them, peace followed. Desire, yes, but also a sense of calm.

He felt her shift, move off the settee and he opened his eye. She had knelt before him and wedged herself between his knees. His heart stuttered at the vision of this woman on her knees, her gaze both warm and wicked as she slid both palms up his thighs, massaging lightly, and then went to work on the buttons of his fall front.

"Ophelia," he ground out through tightly clenched teeth.

She shook her head. "Be quiet, Your Majesty."

He had to laugh at her cheek. God, but she set him on his head. And he liked it. He liked *her* and her warmth and her laughter and her force of nature personality that seemed to wash over him like some kind of tidal wave. He certainly liked it when she finally managed to peel away the front flap of his trousers and free his half-hard cock.

She smiled up at him as she took him in hand, stroking him to full attention with only the slightest effort. He should have stopped her. Should have caught her by her arms and dragged her up his body, but in this moment, coming from such an emotionally charged morning...he couldn't. He wanted this pleasure she offered, this comfort.

Slowly, he let his head drop back against the cushion of the settee, shut his eyes and focused on her touch. And touch she did, the pressure of her fingers increasing slightly as she smoothed her hand over his length. Pleasure followed in the wake of the touch, echoes of it ricocheting throughout his entire body.

But he needed more. He wanted more. Slowly he opened his eyes and found her watching him, her lips wet from licking them, her pupils dilated with the pleasure she was obviously receiving from this act. That she liked it excited him even more.

"Tell me what to do," she whispered.

He swallowed hard. Every gentlemanly instinct told him to shield her from what he wanted. Every animal one demanded he ask for it.

"It is better if it is…wet," he said, his voice rough and low.

Her eyes went slightly wide as she glanced down at his cock. "Oh, like it is inside of me," she whispered.

He groaned because that only made him want more, not less. "Yes, exactly."

She looked up at his face again, her expression unreadable in the firelight. Then she brushed her cheek to his cock. He jolted at both the feel of her satiny skin and the look of her touching him like that. It was such a striking image as she stroked him with her fingers and brushed the head closer and closer to her lips.

At last she darted out her tongue, swirling it around the head of him. He couldn't hold back the strangled moan that followed the intense pleasure such a small act created. She had licked him and it was everything.

She smiled against his cock and then licked him again. Again, wetting the head thoroughly. He waited for her to now use that lubrication in order to stroke him, but she didn't. Instead she took him into her mouth, lightly sucking.

Stars burst before his eyes at the sudden, powerful sensation being multiplied at the most sensitive place in his body. He barked out her name in the quiet, his hand going down to the crown of her head, though whether that was to push her away or hold her where she was, he couldn't say.

She moaned around him, taking him a little deeper. The vibrations shot up his cock and he flexed against her tongue helplessly.

"Thrust," he directed in a strangled tone.

She looked up at him without removing his cock from her mouth. Those beautiful blue eyes were mesmerizing, and she didn't break the gaze as she began to move over him, stroking her mouth up and down his length. He gripped the edge of the settee with one hand, his fingers tangling in her hair with the other.

She might not have much experience in this act, but she had natural talent. She watched him for his response to her every touch and adjusted accordingly. Her hand folded around the base of his cock and he grunted in pleasure. That made her grip tighter as she sucked him, swirling her tongue around him like he was the sweetest treat.

He dropped the hand in her hair, tracing her cheek as she took him, and then caught her wrist. She stopped licking and looked up at him, meeting his stare as he began to move her hand over his base. Her eyes went slightly wide and then she nodded. She wetted his cock more and slid her hand higher to lubricate her palm. Then she went back to sucking him, adding the solid, heavy stroke of her hand to the absolutely life-altering swirl of her tongue.

He found himself pulsing lightly into her mouth, pleasure mounting with every swipe of her tongue, stroke of her hand, with every soft moan she made deep in her throat, like she was as aroused by this as he was.

As she watched him react, she began to increase the pace of her mouth, her tongue swirling faster, her hand pumping with more drive. He found himself grinding into the sensation, pleasure mounting in his balls, racing up his spine, sending spiraling tingles through every inch of his body.

He was going to come—he felt the edge of it growing insistent and wild. He sat up a little and touched her soft hair again, trying to urge her to stop toying with him.

"Ophelia," he gasped. "I'm going to spend."

She lifted her gaze and smiled around his cock before she finally stopped sucking. "I thought that was the point, Grantham."

He managed a strangled laugh at her wicked expression, but when she lowered her head again he caught her chin. "You might not like it in your mouth. Many ladies don't."

She shrugged. "I suppose we'll have to find out."

Without another word, she returned her mouth to him and went back to her work. She took him deeper now, faster, as if his declaration that he would spend was a challenge she intended to win. He arched back as the pleasure built higher, harder, faster, stronger than he had ever felt before. His breath came short, his hips flexed as he took every lick and suck, and finally, the crisis arrived.

"Ophelia," he grunted. "Now!"

He expected her to pull away, but she didn't. He came and she took it, though she didn't swallow, but let the essence of him flow back down over his pulsing cock. His mind emptied with every burst of come, leaving him blissfully relaxed as he flopped back on the settee, boneless and weightless, if only for a moment.

She smiled as she finally released his cock from her lips. She wiped her mouth with the back of her hand, a wicked glint in her eyes. "I don't know about many ladies, but I liked that very much," she said softly.

He caught her arm and drew her up, across his body. He kissed her, tasting himself on her tongue and reveling in the mixture of him and her. God's teeth, but this woman...this remarkable woman...he could scarcely picture what his life had been like before she flounced in and demanded space and time and oh-so-much attention.

He didn't want to go back to the way it had been before. Even though he knew that would happen eventually. There was no stopping it.

~

Ophelia rested her head on Grantham's shoulder, counting every long, steady breath he drew in and out. There was something soothing about this. Oh, her body throbbed with need. Making him come undone had turned out to be the ultimate aphrodisiac. The fact that she could still taste the salty-sweetness of him on her tongue made her body hum all the more.

But there was something so peaceful about having only given to him. Not expecting anything in return. She could see it brought him peace, even if it might be fleeting.

She liked giving him peace.

"You know," she said, lifting her head at last. "I could help."

If she had softened his edges with her tongue, his entire demeanor shifted now. He straightened up, the man shoved under layers of propriety, the king returning as he squeezed her hand gently and got up from the settee. He refastened his trousers, smoothing himself back into place as if the stolen moment had never happened.

She frowned at how easy it was for him.

"You already did help," he said, pivoting back to face her, a false smile on his lips. "Very much."

She wrinkled her brow. "Grantham," she began.

He turned away. "I have so much to do. May we discuss it later? Tonight. You're still joining me tonight?"

She nodded without hesitation. "If you want me, I will be there."

His nostrils flared ever so slightly. "I want you there. Now I must get back to this. You understand."

She got up from the settee, smoothing herself carefully. She checked her hair in the mirror above the fire, adjusting the places where he had mangled her style as she pleasured him. When she turned back, he was already seated at his desk, his expression lined with worry as if what they'd shared had never happened.

"I'll see you later," she said softly as she moved to the door, unlocking it before she opened it.

"Yes." He glanced up, but only barely. "And Ophelia? Thank you."

She inclined her head and exited the room. In the hall, she drew in a shuddering breath. She'd been dismissed rather than invited into his troubles. She was a lover, not a love.

She'd do best to remember that or else risk being hurt.

CHAPTER 15

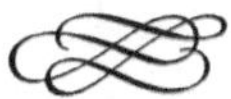

The next time Grantham saw Ophelia was at supper that night. He hadn't wanted to come, but his mother had insisted, all but dragging him to the table to sit with his family. They were trying to make this better and he appreciated it, but all their idle chatter didn't work. It was just noise, a background to his worries… and his desires.

It was odd to have the two combined. To have such a weight pressing to his chest but then to look down the table to Ophelia, smiling at something his brother had said, and feel the throb of need, as well…

It made a man's head spin.

She glanced down at him, as if she sensed his attention on her. She smiled slightly, though her brow wrinkled like she could read his troubles without effort. How had that happened?

She cleared her throat. "I had a question, if the family is up to answering."

The queen smiled at her. "Of course. Ask away."

"Well, having been a close observer of your family for weeks, I have surmised that Prince Remington is surely the wild one of your family."

Remi snorted before he took a long drink of wine. "Don't under-estimate the queen, my dear."

"Remi!" Giabella burst out, and laughed long and hard. Grantham couldn't help but smile. Remi had always been able to make their mother's mask of propriety slip. "Do not reveal state secrets at the supper table."

Next to her, Dash bent his head, smothering a smile as the rest of them laughed. Giabella glanced at him, and again Grantham saw their connection. Once all this chaos was resolved, perhaps he would have to speak to her about what he had observed. She deserved to be happy, after all.

Ophelia laughed. "I would never ask for state secrets, Your Majesty," she said, but then she shook her head. "But then again, perhaps I am. Because my question is…what is the wildest thing King Grantham ever did?"

Grantham tilted his head and speared her with a glance, his worries peeling away, yet again. "You assume I have ever been wild, my lady?"

She met his stare and held. "I guarantee it, Your Majesty."

He blinked as he realized the table had gone silent and everyone was watching the exchange. Bollocks, he was going to cock this up and drag his entire family into it with their loud and unceasing opinions.

He held up his hands. "Are there any suggestions?" he asked. "Ilaria is not here to offer hers, but I'm sure the rest of you have your thoughts. I give full permission to reveal the family secrets."

Remi snorted again. "That might take all night."

Sasha arched a brow at Grantham. "I could tell the story about the time you stole the apples."

Giabella straightened up at the head of the table. "Apples?" she repeated.

Grantham shook his head and chuckled. "You just couldn't wait to tattle to Mama."

"After fifteen years, Grantham!" Sasha protested. "And I was certain you knew, Mama." The queen shook her head and Sasha took a big gulp of wine before she began, "Now, to be fair, the apples did go to the orphans, so perhaps we should call it a Robin Hood tale."

Grantham smiled as Ophelia leaned forward, eyes wide as Sasha told the story of an overturned applecart, a very cruel guard and the future King of Athawick giving the apples to some orphans while Remi distracted the rest.

When she was finished, Giabella told a story of when he was young and used to play tricks of the courtiers. No one named Blairford, but the reminder that he'd always been a thorn in that man's side was helpful. Finally Remi told a rather bawdier tale of a state visit to their mother's home country of Everlay and a party that made Ophelia blush.

By the time they were finished, the family was laughing, as was Grantham, and Ophelia was shaking her head. "I take it all back—I think your most troublesome family member is the king after all."

Grantham laughed. "I think you've believed that since the first moment you met me, admit it now, my lady!"

She folded her arms. "I shall admit nothing, not even under torture."

He arched a brow, thinking of all the delicious ways he could torture this woman later. He cleared his throat. "Why don't we make our way to the parlor for a drink, yes?"

The rest agreed and he smiled at Ophelia before he got up and moved to take his mother's arm as was proper. They walked together to the parlor where drinks awaited. His mother glanced up at him. "I was so pleased to see you smile tonight," she said. "You have so much weighing on your heart and mind—that you could have some of it lifted is very good. Something I fully support."

Grantham sighed as they entered the parlor. He moved to the sideboard and prepared his mother a sherry. As he handed it over, he said, "What would take the weight fully from my shoulders is doing what will better the country." He glanced toward Ophelia, chatting with Dash at the window. Her bright smile glowing as usual. "That is all I can think about in whatever future decisions I make."

Giabella's expression fell as she reached out to touch Grantham's hand. "My love, it will work out. I promise you."

"I know," he said, thrusting his shoulders back. "Because I will put in all the work I can to ensure it. Now let us talk of something else, shall we?"

His mother nodded and they did so, but he couldn't help letting his gaze drift to Ophelia again. Tonight he would give himself the respite she offered once again. Despite everything, he would take it as long as he could.

But he could never forget that the time spent with her could only be brief.

Ophelia stood outside the ornately painted door that led to the king's chamber and hesitated. Grantham had asked her to join him here. His looks that lingered ever longer as the evening ended told her he still desired her company. And she certainly desired his. His touch was all she could think about.

But knocking still felt like a huge step. Something she could never take back, something that would yet again change the dynamic between them and leave her on unsteady footing as she tried to determine what this was and how to keep from destroying herself in trade for earthshaking pleasure.

"For God's sake," she muttered at last, and rapped her knuckles against the door.

As if he were waiting there, Grantham opened the door immediately. He wore no jacket, no waistcoat. His cravat was gone, his shirtsleeves rolled to the elbow. He was barefoot. She sucked in a breath at his appearance, though she wasn't sure why the sight made her heart race so. It wasn't as if she hadn't seen him undone. In the library they'd been naked together, for heaven's sake. But this felt so casual, so vulnerable.

They were truly lovers. There was a comfort between them that meant he could strip out of more than clothing, but also the formal persona he wore as king.

"You are staring," he said, catching her hand and drawing her into the room. "An inauspicious start."

She smiled and looked around the room as he shut the door behind him. They were in the antechamber, and it was massive. A place where he could meet with family or servants. There was a desk on one side of the room, a smaller version of the one he had in his study. Before the fire was a settee and two chairs, all positioned to face the warmth. The walls were papered. There was an intricate carved ceiling with images of boats on the sea.

"Goodness," she breathed. "You really *are* the king."

He choked out a laugh and she glanced at him. When she found him grinning at her, her breath caught again. He was hardly ever so expressive and it made him so much more handsome. It was rather unfair that it was possible.

"I am, or so they say," he said. "I will admit, I'm still growing accustomed to the room. After all, I inherited it from the previous occupant after his death."

She nodded. "Of course."

He looked around and his brow wrinkled. "I tried to convince my mother that she should keep it. After all, her old chamber was just through that door there." He motioned to a door on the right side of the antechamber. "But I think she was just as happy to leave her own unpleasant memories behind and start anew."

"They weren't happy together," Ophelia said softly.

He shook his head. "They were not."

"It doesn't surprise me. Your mother is so kind, so wonderful, I cannot imagine her being a good fit based on your description of your father."

"No," he agreed, then ran a hand through his hair. "And now...

well, I've begun to notice things that make me question all I've believed."

"Such as?" she asked, moving toward him.

Although she actually trembled with anticipation of what they would do in this beautiful room and the likely even more beautiful bedchamber she assumed was through the left side door, she liked this easy connection. She liked that there was no sense of rush.

He sighed. "I think my mother may...care for someone else. Perhaps she has for a very long time."

"Mr. Talbot?" Ophelia asked gently.

His eyes went wide. "Now how could you notice it after an acquaintance of weeks when I didn't see it, even though Dash has worked for my mother for over a decade?"

She pondered the question. "I suppose it is like all things when we are close to them. We don't notice the tiny changes. For example, if I cut just the slightest bit off my hair and I did it every day or every other day, you might not notice until it was very short. But if someone saw a portrait where my hair was long and then saw me after I'd been cutting it a few weeks, they might make note of its length."

"I rather like your hair as it is, my lady."

She laughed. "And I have no intentions of changing it, I assure you. In this case, you might have seen the little changes between you mother and her secretary over the years and their relationship just feels...normal. As it always has been. But when I walk in, I mark their closeness differently. The way he...the way he looks at her when she isn't attending." She swallowed and forced herself to look away from him now. This conversation felt like it wasn't just about his mother. "The way she blushes if he grazes her hand."

He said nothing, but closed the distance between them in a few long steps. He caught her hand, tangling his fingers with hers. She glanced down and they stared together at the clasped hands. Then she slowly looked up into his face and her breath grew shaky because being near him always threw her entire being off balance.

"Do you think she would allow herself to...to explore that connection?" she asked.

"I don't know. Her position, her past...they make things difficult."

"Not just for her," she said softly.

"My father was cruel," he said. "I already told you that. Perhaps none of us learned how to love easily."

"And yet your siblings have all found their matches and are happy," she whispered. "So you must have hope for her...for you."

"But the expectations are so different for me," he said, and now he released her hand and stepped away. She felt the distance keenly. "I cannot only pursue what I...what I want, can I?"

"Perhaps not forever, but for a little while."

He sighed and scrubbed a hand through his hair. "Yes, I suppose that is true. These small breaks do help me carry the weight that is mine and mine alone."

She stared at him and for the first time realized just how isolated he was. Yes, because he created scenarios where he forced that. He distanced himself from people. He allowed himself to be an institution before he was a man.

But also because it was true that he was uniquely alone. As king, he had to shoulder the weight by himself. Passing it off was always only temporary. The loneliness of that fact pierced her like it was a blade and she was overwhelmed by a desire to help. To ease. To commiserate.

She took his hand again. He let her and smiled down at her.

"May I tell you something?"

He nodded slowly. "Anything."

She felt heat flooding her cheeks and sucked in a breath in the hopes it would calm her. It didn't work. His expression grew concerned and he guided her to the settee before the fire. They sat there together, hands entangled against his thigh.

"Tell me," he said gently.

"When I confessed to you about Erasmus...I...I left something out." She hated how her voice cracked. "Even Priscilla doesn't know."

"What is it?"

"After everything happened, after I found out the truth, I...I thought I might be with child." Tears jumped to her eyes at the memory.

He caught his breath. "Oh no."

She nodded. "For weeks, I had no idea what to do. My brother had shuttled me off to the country, I was terrified because the consequences would have been so dire. So for weeks I waited and hoped and feared. I looked into healers who might help me handle the situation if it came to that. And then..." She shook her head. "Then my courses came. There was no baby."

"You must have been relieved," he said.

"Entirely relieved, yes. And I know it isn't the same as what you must feel. But during those horrible weeks I was completely alone. I couldn't bring anyone into my terror, I had to think and plan and fear all alone."

He stared down at her. "It is the same. And no, my duties and all that comes with them cannot be alleviated so simply, but I do appreciate that you have felt what I feel. That weight that is like a house being pressed down on you."

"Yes. Or a palace. Or a country." She reached up and traced his cheek with her fingertips, reveling in the hint of scratchy stubble that reminded her he was a man, not a statue in a garden. He was real and he was here with her, no matter how short their time was. "Can I help you relieve it?"

"I would very much like that."

He leaned in, gliding his fingers into her hair. She shivered as the pins loosened, slid free, and her locks fell around his hands, tangling and looping them together. She lifted her mouth and closed her eyes, waiting for his kiss, but it never came. At last, she opened one eye.

"If you just lean in, Your Majesty, and press your mouth to mine, it is called a kiss," she said, reverting to teasing because he looked so thoughtful.

He snorted a laugh. "Oh yes, I do recall, my lady. But I was just thinking that every time we have done this, it has been perched precariously on a settee. And I would like to finally bed you in my actual bed. So will you come with me?"

She nodded, rising when he rose, following as he took her to the doorway on the left side of the antechamber and through it as he opened it. Once again, she caught her breath. This room was bigger than the last. Dominated by a huge bed against the wall, facing the window. Even in the darkness of the middle of the night, she saw the moonlight reflected on the sea far below.

"Beautiful," she murmured.

He drew her to his chest, and this time he did kiss her. "Oh yes, you are."

She shivered. This man was such a dichotomy. He could frustrate her and arouse her, sometimes in the same breath. He left her challenged and needy whenever they were near each other. And she wanted nothing more than to have that feeling for as long as she could.

She wrapped her arms around his neck and the kiss deepened, slow at first, but growing in intensity and desperation the longer it went on. His fingers dug into her hair again and he tilted her face up, making her look at him. His expression was dark, filled with desire, hungry for her, and her entire body reacted to that rarely seen side of this man.

"I'm going to make you come, Ophelia," he whispered, his voice harsh. "I'm going to do that over and over again until you are weak with it. Until you don't remember anything but my name."

She nodded, the action restricted by his grip against her hair. "Yes," she whimpered, giving herself over completely, knowing she might not ever get everything back in the end. "Yes, yes, please yes."

CHAPTER 16

Ophelia felt the shift in Grantham the moment she said yes, giving her full and enthusiastic permission for whatever he wanted to do to her. His movement became animal, hard, intoxicating, and his gaze more focused.

He didn't speak, but spun her around, pulling her backside against his pelvis, grinding the very hard cock she now felt against her. She gasped at the feeling, at the swift and efficient way he stripped the buttons along her spine open. He shoved the dress forward, trapping her arms in the fabric before he leaned into her, arching her back as he kissed her neck, down the line of her spine through her chemise.

"God, you smell good," he groaned against her shoulder. "I shall never forget it."

She smiled, then gasped as he caught her chemise strap with his teeth and began to drag it down. He traced his way back up with his tongue, kissing and sucking and teasing all the way. Pleasure followed, heated and powerful. It was such a strange thing to realize that her entire body was his instrument, not just her sex or her breasts or her mouth. Every part of her responded to him, as if she had been sleeping and only he could wake her.

He tugged the other chemise strap down with his fingers as he kissed the side of her neck. She ground back against him, breath shortening, and he chuckled against her skin.

"The things you do to me," he grunted. "I always knew you were trouble."

Now she laughed, though it was shaky, shakier still when he pulled the dress and underthings away to bunch at her waist and pressed each of her hands on the edge of the mattress. She leaned forward, presenting herself as he clearly desired.

"I knew it," she teased. "From the moment you met me, I knew you didn't like me."

"I liked you fine," he drawled. "I liked you too much. I said you were trouble, *that* is different."

His hands moved as he spoke, sliding down her back and sides with firm pressure, under what was left of her gown. He let it pool at her feet and she kicked it away. Now she was just in her stockings and slippers, her backside bare.

He hesitated and she looked over her shoulder to find him staring at her, eyes wide, as if he had never seen her…never seen any woman…before. She circled her hips slowly, loving how his pupils dilated with desire, how he extended his shaking hands and cupped her hips, pulling her back possessively.

He massaged there gently, his thumbs tracing her backside, lower and lower, until he was spreading her lightly, opening her. She widened her stance, lifting herself and knowing she was lewdly presenting her sex like an animal in heat.

Not the worst comparison. Certainly she felt heated. She wanted what he could offer. She wanted everything. He gave it, moving one hand between her legs, stroking her gently.

She shivered, dropping her head down, closing her eyes to focus on the sensation. He massaged, the perfect pressure against her outer lips, the teasing dip past them. She ground back, her fingers gripping the coverlet, her moans and his ragged breath the only sound in the quiet.

"Turn around," he whispered, his mouth close to her ear.

She did, and found her back pressed hard into the edge of the mattress. He leaned in to kiss her mouth and she lifted into him with a needy whimper. He plundered her and she loved it. Loved that he was as lost as she was. Loved that he wanted her so much that he could forget who he was, even for a moment.

When he pulled his mouth from hers, she reached for him, but he would not be brought back. Instead he slowly sank to his knees, kissing a path down the apex of her body as he did so. When he looked up at her, she nearly buckled. "There is something so intoxicating about having a king on his knees before me," she said softly.

His cheek twitched. "This king will always go to his knees for you. Now open your legs."

She did so, blushing as he leaned in so his face was tantalizingly close to her sex. He nuzzled her inner thigh with his cheek, abrading the sensitive skin lightly. "Wider."

She huffed out a breath and did so, clutching the edge of the mattress. "It isn't exactly easy."

He cupped her thigh and maneuvered her, draping her leg over his shoulder. "Better?" he asked as he pressed his mouth to her. The word vibrated against her clitoris and she gasped.

"Yes!"

He smiled against her and then began to lick, just as he had on the throne the day before, just as he had on the settee in the library. She pressed back against the mattress, grinding against him as he lavished her with long licks and quick sucks. He was teasing her, far more than he had either time before. Of course, he could. They were locked in his chamber—no one would dare interrupt them.

He had all night to do this. He seemed to wish to use it to torture because he brought her to the edge of release and then just...kept her there. For what felt like an eternity. Over and over, he let her feel the first flutters of release and then he would back off until she was squirming and cursing and glaring down at him.

"Have I ever told you how much I despise you?" she grunted.

He smiled up at her, then went right back to licking. "I had a feeling," he murmured between swipes of his tongue. "Do you want this?" He punctuated the question by sucking her clitoris with purpose.

She cried out his name. "Yes!"

"Will you ask for it?"

"Please," she gasped, trying to chase the tongue he moved away. "Please let me."

His eyes came up, dark and dangerous, and then he sucked her hard and fast, swirling his tongue around the hard ridge of her clitoris. The orgasm hit her so hard, so fast, that she nearly fell over. It was nothing like she'd experienced before, like her whole body rolled with the sensation, like she had left the ground and was flying. He cupped her hips to keep her still, potentially to avoid a broken nose as she flexed wildly and kept torturing her until she was spent and gasping.

Only then did he lift his head, licking his slick lips with a smugly satisfied expression before he rose up and kissed her deeply. She tasted her release on his tongue, his lips, and drank of it greedily.

"Let's try that again," he said, lifting her onto the edge of the bed and pushing his hips between her legs.

"Only if you remove some clothes," she said, tugging at his shirt.

He nodded and stepped back, pulling the shirt over his head with one arm. She gasped, just as she had before, at how beautiful he was. Would that ever stop? Would she ever look at his body and not be impressed and aroused? She doubted it.

Those thoughts faded as he unfastened his trousers and slipped them off, kicking it all away to join the pile of her things.

"Far more fair," she said, reaching for him, loving the slide of her hands over his bare skin. "Now we're both naked."

"Not quite," he said, nodding toward her legs.

She smiled. Her stockings and garters were hardly a full ball gown, but if he could torture, so could she. She slid back on the bed, resting her head on the pillows, and then made a show of sliding her hands down her body. Touching herself wasn't just torture for him, but she ignored the answering call of pleasure and watched him shift at her performance.

She unbuttoned the first garter and tossed it away, then began to roll her silk stocking down slowly. She tossed it toward him as she repeated the same action on her other leg. When she was finished and truly naked, he held up the first stocking, smoothing it to its full length.

"You know, I could do some very wicked things to you with these."

Her eyes went wide. "Like what?"

"They'd made excellent ties," he said. "I'm sure I could find a spot on the bedpost to fasten them to. And then I could truly tease you all night."

She shivered at the idea. "But what if I have plans for my hands and arms?"

He arched a brow and threw the stocking over his shoulder before he crawled onto the bed beside her. "Then we save the stockings for next time."

She smiled at the idea that there would be a next time. She wanted so many more next times. She wanted to explore this man's body and find all the angles of his pleasure until they were both spent, even if it took weeks, months, years…a lifetime.

She shook that thought away. She didn't have any of those units of time left with him. So she had best enjoy what she had and not make plans that would only be destroyed.

She reached for him, raking her nails along his back as he covered her with his body. God, his weight was delicious now that she felt the full measure of it. The bed had been a remarkable idea.

His mouth found hers and they kissed once more. All the while he touched her, like he couldn't get enough of her skin. Like he was trying to memorize every curve of her body. She wanted him to do just that. She wanted to be seared on his mind forever.

"Please," she whispered, forcing a hand between them and sliding it to find his cock. She stroked him and then rubbed him against her entrance.

He lifted his head and stared down at her, his expression unreadable. Then he slid forward, taking her body inch by inch, filling her entirely as she lifted to force him faster. When he was fully seated, he rested his forehead to hers, locking their gazes, and began to move gently.

She realized almost instantly that he was rocking against her in a way designed to toy with her, just as he had done with his tongue. He stimulated her clitoris with every roll of his hips and yet only drew her back to the very edge of pleasure, did not let her fall.

And all the time he watched her, adjusting to her every gasp and rake of her nails across his back. He held her stare and poured himself into her, all his strength and power focused on her pleasure. This man who could move mountains, change worlds, snap his fingers and have what he desired…he focused on *her*.

That realization pushed her over the edge he had been denying. She rose up against him, sucking his lower lip, scratching his back as rippling waves of pleasure overtook her. After her first orgasm, this one was deeper and more powerful, like an earthquake that shifted every part of her.

He smiled against her mouth. "Trust you to simply take what you want."

"I'll steal it if you won't give it," she gasped, flopping back. "But I promise to give you something in return."

"You already do," he said softly.

"Roll on your back?" she asked.

He hesitated, but then he did so, gripping her to him as he shifted so that their bodies never parted. She adjusted herself, tightening her knees around his midsection, resting one hand against his broad shoulder and gripping the headboard with the other.

Slowly she began to grind, riding him. He captured her hips, staring up at her, wide eyed as she took him, used him for her pleasure, drew out his own. She was shocked that as they rocked together, she felt the tingling heat of yet another orgasm. It seemed he would keep his earlier promise about making her come over and over until she forgot everything but him.

In that moment, he was all that existed already.

She bucked harder and then dropped her hands to his chest, rocking through the pleasure, gasping when he sat up and wrapped his arms around her. He lifted against her as his mouth found hers, increasing the pleasure once more, drawing it out like he did with such effortless talent.

When she had stopped writhing he rolled them over again, back on top, his arms still tightly around her. He buried his head into the crook of her neck, thrusting faster now, harder. The edge of his control was right there, a thread that had been drawn tight…then too tight…by every touch. She wanted to break it. To watch as he convulsed with pleasure the same way she had. She cupped his bare backside, urging him faster. He grunted against her neck and then cried out, pulling from her, his release splashing between them in a glorious mess of pleasure and heat and connection.

He collapsed, breath hard, and she wrapped her arms as tightly around him as she could, holding him against her, never wanting the moment to come when he was parted from her.

And knowing that was impossible, because the moment was always waiting, too close on the horizon. One day she would reach it and then this dream would end.

Grantham's entire body felt heavy as he rolled away from Ophelia at last. He shifted to his side to face her and she did the same. They were silent for a while, both just staring at each other as the weight of what had just happened sank in.

He had made love plenty of times in his thirty years. Remi would say not nearly enough, but pleasure had never been a stranger to Grantham, even if it hadn't been a recent visitor.

But he had never felt anything like what he'd just experienced with Ophelia. Not with any other person, not on any other night. The connection he'd felt was intense and powerful, not something he could pretend away, no matter how much he wanted to.

He smoothed her hair away from her face and she smiled at him softly. The truth of it was so clear and so powerful, so easy and yet so ungodly hard: he was in love with her.

There was no surprise at the realization. It was as easy as breathing to recognize it and know it was true. He loved Ophelia. There had been some part of him on that path for as long as he'd known her. From the first moment that he'd stepped into a parlor and been utterly astounded by the chaotic angel he'd found there.

The more he'd come to know her, especially in the weeks they'd been in Athawick, had only made that feeling grow. Bloom and spread to touch every single part of his life.

He wished he could celebrate that. He wished he could surrender to it as his siblings had. Watching them embrace their happiness had been one of the greatest joys of his life, and here he was, looking into the face of his own truest happiness and...

Well, he couldn't embrace it. He couldn't pull her close and whisper the words that would change them both. He couldn't pick some beautiful ring from the royal collection and slip it on her finger and a crown on her head and call her his queen.

Because the world he ruled was not well. It was, if he admitted it to himself, in chaos. And while Ophelia, herself, was sometimes chaos, he couldn't drag her into the mess his life was going to be. He couldn't ask her to give up who she was, what she was, and become the queen of an uneasy nation. To do so would be to break her...and definitely put her in danger.

"You are suddenly sad," she whispered.

He smiled despite himself. Of course she would see that truth. She'd been seeing through him for as long as he'd known her. Frustrating hoyden that she was. Beautiful angel.

"Perhaps it is because I know that morning will come," he lied. "And then this night will be over."

She nodded solemnly. "But you know the most wonderful thing?"

"No, what is that?"

She leaned in and kissed him. Gently, but with promise and purpose that impossibly stirred his depleted body back to life. "Tonight isn't over yet," she whispered.

He didn't answer, but dragged her closer, slipping her beneath him as he drowned in all the beauty and passion she had to offer. Soon enough he would have to come up for air.

And once he did, he would never be truly happy again, because she would take some part of him with her when she left. So he had to revel in her now, revel in being whole in her arms and forget, for just a little while longer, that the pain that was coming was going to be devastating.

CHAPTER 17

"I don't have time for this," Grantham said the next morning as he strode into the parlor to which Remi had called him. His tone was, perhaps, a bit more annoyed than he wished it to be. But he was tired, thanks to his night with Ophelia. One that had only ended a few short hours before when she'd slipped from his bed with one last searing kiss.

And he'd spent the following few hours wondering if it might be the last. So Remi's demand that he join him was not met with as much grace as he probably should have expressed.

He skidded to a stop as he saw his brother. Remi was stripped down to the waist, trousers slung low on his hips and his hands were wrapped with cloth, protecting his knuckles. The furniture had been removed from this little-used room and now it looked as it once had years ago when they had used it as their boxing ring and fencing piste.

"Remi," Grantham said, troubles pushed aside for the moment as he fully entered the room. "What did you do?"

His brother grinned and held up his arms as he made a slow turn. "Returned the room to what it was originally, of course. Father took it away as punishment for…God, I don't even know what."

Grantham turned his head. Remi didn't recall because the punishment hadn't been his, for once. Their father had taken this room away from them because of something *Grantham* had done.

"It's going to be a long day," Remi said, this time a bit more gently. "And you and I may not be as…as close as we once were, but I'm not so selfish that I can't see the pain on your face. I know you're suffering."

Grantham pursed his lips. "Don't be ridiculous."

Remi snorted. "Still have to leave those walls up, do you? Very well, that's your prerogative as king. If I annoy you by pressing, why don't you solve the problem in the boxing ring?"

Grantham stared past him at the square in the middle of the room that would serve as a ring. His hands itched at the idea of shrugging off propriety, at having a physical release. After all, the physical release with Ophelia was certainly helping. In those moments with her, he could almost forget the inevitability of his life.

"Fine," he said. "But I really do have other matters to attend. I can't spend an inordinate amount of time doing this with you."

Remi chuckled as Grantham began to strip out of his jacket and unwind his cravat. "Oh, well, thank you very much, Your Majesty. I appreciate you making time in your schedule."

Grantham huffed out his breath, but he was trying to cover a laugh. He set aside his jacket, his cravat, his vest, his linen shirt. Remi produced the strips to wrap his knuckles and then went to work protecting Grantham's hands with the bindings.

"Who wrapped yours?" Grantham asked, motioning his head toward his brother's own hands.

Remi smiled, his gaze a little wicked as he lifted it. "Priscilla, of course," he said. "Though it did take a few times to…er…focus."

Grantham rolled his eyes, but there was a hollow feeling in his chest. His brother, the rambling rake who had never taken anything in his life seriously, had found a woman who appeared to be his perfect match. Priscilla accepted Remi, and she made him better.

Grantham saw that even in the short time they had known each other, the shorter time they had been married.

He found himself thinking about Ophelia. She continued to try to reach out to him. To offer her support and assistance, and all he was able to do was push her away. Create a bubble for himself where no one could reach him, no one could help him.

Wasn't that what his father had taught him, after all? That as king he was responsible for everything and that if he asked for help it only made him weak?

Remi didn't seem weak to him now that he'd opened himself up.

"That is a sour look," Remi said, tying and tucking the last piece of wrap so that both his hands were protected. "Why don't you work out whatever caused it in the ring?"

They moved into the center of the room together and Grantham extended his hand into the center so they could bump their knuckles together. A reminder that this was a friendly match. Sparring, not fighting.

They squared off, circling each other slowly. Remi was smiling, Grantham was not. He was too focused to smile, searching for the opening that Remi would eventually give. When his brother moved just a touch too lazily, he took advantage, shooting his fist out and connecting, albeit lightly, to Remi's cheek.

"Nicely done," Remi encouraged.

Grantham ignored him and threw another blow. Remi dodged, but Grantham still felt his knuckles brush along his brother's ribcage.

"Excellent shot," Remi said. "You've always had a good right."

They continued on like that for a few more minutes. Grantham connecting, Remi encouraging with each blow. At last, Grantham lowered his hands and his brow. "Are you fighting me or are you here for some other reason?"

The flicker of Remi's gaze as he darted it away was answer enough. Was it pity? God damn, but Grantham wasn't going to accept that. The very thought of it brought anger up in his chest.

Anger at so many things. He pushed Remi with the flat of his palms.

"Hit me," he ordered. Remi hesitated and Grantham shoved him again. "Fucking hit me."

Remi pursed his lips. "We're sparring. I'm not going to hit you."

"I want you to," Grantham admitted, and heard the words echo in the empty room around him. Heard the desperation he couldn't keep out of his tone. He bent his head. "I don't want to feel, I want to bleed."

Remi's expression twisted at that admission and the pain on his brother's face hit Grantham in the chest as hard as any fist might have. He and Remi had once been so close, and they had been torn apart by the past few years as their father grew ill, as Grantham's responsibilities weighed heavier and he was pulled further and further into becoming an institution and away from being a man. He'd felt Remi's mounting resentment in that time. They had even come to blows…real blows…not ten days before when things with Priscilla had reached a boiling point.

But right now Grantham saw none of that tangled history. He only saw his brother and all the love they had once shared with each other. He saw it there, as strong as ever and it nearly buckled him.

"I'm not going to make you bleed," Remi said softly. "But if you need to fight, I'll fight."

Grantham nodded and they squared off again. This time he felt the difference in his brother's stance, in his look. And when they met in the middle of the ring, they were now evenly matched. They swung, connecting lightly, but still hard enough that it hurt. Both of them made a point of avoiding the face as much as possible. After all, they had official duties to attend to in a few hours. But the body connections took Grantham's air at times and did exactly as he had wanted them to.

They made him forget.

Only it was imperfect. The responsibilities drifted away, but as he began to tire from the exertion, the emotion remained. Multiplied somehow without all the thoughts and duties to consider. He was bombarded by it all, overwhelmed. Love for Ophelia and the hopelessness of that. Fear for his future, for the ways he had already failed and the ways he still would. Anger at Blairford and his father and…and himself. Always himself. Mostly at himself.

He swung wild and Remi easily dodged him as Grantham lost his balance in his upset. His brother pivoted and caught him, arms around his waist to keep him from hitting the floor.

Grantham should have stepped away. Pushed away and carried on, but he couldn't. Instead, he buckled against his brother, letting out his breath in a long and jagged sigh of pain. Remi's arms tightened around him, even when Grantham tried with his last surge of energy to shrug away.

Then he did collapse and was shocked to find tears streaming down his face. Remi sank to the ground with him, still holding him in the tightest hug Grantham had probably ever experienced. He allowed it, draped half across his brother like he was a child as he wept.

The outburst didn't last long. He couldn't allow that. After a moment, he sucked in a few long breaths, calming himself. Remi's hold loosened and Grantham sat up, wiping the tears from his cheeks. They stared at each other.

"It's a great deal to carry, Grantham," his brother said softly.

Grantham didn't answer that charge. It was too difficult and he didn't want to lose control of himself again. "You…you couldn't recall why Father took the boxing area from us as children."

Remi tilted his head. "You do?"

Grantham jerked out an unsteady nod. "It was because I confronted him about his mistress. One of the ones he used to keep here in the palace. I'd found Mama crying, I overheard her say something about it. So I confronted him."

Remi blinked. "I-I had no idea you had done that."

"He was so enraged that I would dare do so," Grantham continued. "I thought he might actually kill me. He locked me in the tower instead."

Remi's brow wrinkled and then understanding dawned. "The tower. *My* tower?"

Grantham sighed. He'd fought so hard to keep this to himself, but now it felt right to share it. Ophelia had opened him up enough that he could. "He used to do that. Many times. It's why I closed the tower up after his death."

Remi shook his head. "Great God, no wonder you had such a strong reaction to my taking Priscilla there. I'm sorry, Grantham. We can move out of the—"

"No," Grantham interrupted. "Please don't. Once I wanted you to. I was even ready to confront you about it. But Ophelia…" He hesitated. "Ophelia made me see that your happiness in that place helps to temper my unhappiness. It transforms it into a good part of our home. And I would not take that from you."

Remi held his stare. "Ophelia, eh?"

Grantham began to unwrap his hands slowly rather than answer. It didn't stop Remi from carrying on.

"You've spent a great deal of time with Ophelia recently. Perhaps a bit more than you wish to say."

Grantham snorted. "I assume Ophelia has told Priscilla that we are lovers? And that she did not keep that fact from you."

Remi's eyes went wide. "Little minx did not tell me that."

"Bloody hell," Grantham muttered. So much for keeping his secrets. It seemed he would spill them all now that the floodgates were open.

"Of course, we have been a bit busy preparing for this last-minute presentation and perhaps Priscilla didn't feel it was her secret to tell."

"Here you've forced it out of me regardless," Grantham grumbled.

"Hardly." Remi chuckled. "You surrendered the information quite easily. I didn't even have to employ torture tactics."

"Only your company." They laughed together a moment. Then Grantham bent his head. "Well, now you know. I'm sure you have a great many thoughts that you won't keep to yourself."

"You were never the kind to take casual lovers," Remi said, his tone careful, as if he weren't sure of the response he would receive. "Does that mean this is something more?"

Grantham sucked in a breath. He loved Ophelia. He knew that as much now as he had known it the previous night as they lay in each other's arms. And yet the situation was still helpless.

"I don't know that it can be," he said softly. "There are many barriers in the way, after all. I'm not free to do whatever I wish."

"If you could?" Remi pressed.

Grantham opened and shut his mouth. "Perhaps it's better I don't travel that particular road, brother. It seems the path of heartache."

He slowly pushed to his feet and extended a hand to Remi to help him up from the floor. To his surprise, Remi tugged him in for yet another hug, though this time it was briefer and somewhat less emotional.

"I watched you push away so much of yourself thanks to Father," Remi said as they broke apart. "But he's gone now, Grantham. *You* get to decide who you are as a leader and who you are as a man. I hope you'll include happiness in both those equations."

Grantham flinched and backed away. "A king's happiness must come from the comfort of his people. Of all the things Father taught, that is the one good lesson. I must find a way to resign myself to it."

Remi's brow wrinkled and Grantham could see he wished to argue further on the point. To avoid it, he stepped back. "Now, it is getting late. Only a few hours to the presentation on the terrace. I should ready myself."

Remi inclined his head and let Grantham go. He pushed his shoulders back as he did so, trying to recall that he was king. And that had to take precedence over all else.

~

Ophelia sat on a chair in Priscilla's dressing room watching as she was carefully dressed in a beautiful gown. Sasha and Queen Giabella were standing to the side, picking through case after case of beautiful jewels and crowns that had been brought for the occasion. From time to time, Priscilla would glance at them in a rather worried way.

At last, Ophelia got to her feet and stepped up, smiling at the fussing maids. The young women seemed to understand and hustled away. Ophelia met Priscilla's gaze in the full-length mirror before her. "You're nervous?"

Priscilla let out her breath in a shaky laugh. "How could one not be? I'm about to be presented as Remi's bride. A princess, for heaven's sake. And if that weren't enough, this announcement is meant to take pressure off the rumors surrounding the departure of Blairford. It's all very important. I don't want to let the family down. Or Remi. Most of all Remi."

Ophelia slid an arm around her. "Remi adores you. You could burn the palace down to the cinders and he would beam and say you were a marvel. Disappointing him is not an outcome you shall ever find yourself handling."

Priscilla laughed and some of the tension left her face. "I hope you're right. Oh, I wish you could stand on the terrace with us. I've been told hundreds will be welcomed through the palace gates, perhaps even a thousand or more. To know you were standing beside me..."

Ophelia shook her head. "The point of this exercise is to quiet whispers, not start them. If I were to stand on the terrace, there would be questions. After all, I don't belong there."

She said the words and they tasted very bitter after the past few days as Grantham's lover. Last night, especially, had made her feel so close to him. But morning light reminded her it was an illusion.

She forced brightness and continued, "But I will be in the

antechamber behind the formal terrace, watching it all. You will feel my support from there, I know."

"Are you certain you don't belong?" Priscilla asked, glancing toward the queen and Sasha. Her voice dropped to a whisper. "I still think there is a place for you here."

Ophelia sighed but was pleased she didn't have to respond when the others approached, their hands draped in jewels to try with Priscilla's gown. The excitement of that moment pushed the rest away. Ophelia concentrated on the fun of it, but in the background, her pain still niggled, a constant reminder that whether or not Priscilla accepted it, Ophelia had no place in this world.

And soon enough the pretense that she did would be gone and she would go with it.

CHAPTER 18

Grantham looked around the antechamber that led to the formal terrace at the front of the palace. It was a smallish parlor, finely decorated for the moments when it was needed for matters of state. Otherwise, it was rarely used. Today, though, it was filled with his entire family, save Jonah and Ilaria, who were still gone to Southern Athawick. A letter from Jonah had arrived that very morning, saying they were still trying to make arrangements to meet with the leader of the opposition.

But otherwise, the rest were there, all dressed in their court finery. His mother fussed over Priscilla, adjusting her crown, speaking softly to her to help ease her nerves. Remi had never looked more regal, standing at attention, his hand clasped in his bride's.

Sasha and Thomas stood to the side, talking softly together. Grantham was proud at how swiftly they had readied themselves for this event. Prouder still of the staff and Dash, who had created something special and made certain the public garden below the terrace was filled with subjects and the dignitaries they could rush here on short notice.

It was obvious they were making a desperation play, perhaps. But no one had ever done it better.

He was about to speak to the family when the parlor door opened and Dash entered, followed by Ophelia. Grantham's words died on his lips. She was also formally dressed, though she would not join them on the terrace for the family presentation. She couldn't, of course, but God's teeth, he wished she could. She smiled at him softly, then shifted that bright expression to Priscilla as she and Dash took up a place away from the family group.

The buglers were entering the terrace now from a secret door on the side of the parapet and the crowd below grew quieter as they blared out the sound of announcement. Grantham took a long breath and then stepped out first into the bright sunshine of this autumn day.

His mother followed, then Sasha and Thomas. The last were Remi and Priscilla, and when they appeared the crowd applauded enthusiastically. The couple waved, and from so far below, Grantham was certain no one noticed how Priscilla's hand shook. Remi did, of course, and settled a hand at the base of her back. When he did, Priscilla straightened, confidence entering her expression.

Grantham smiled at the warm connection between his brother and Priscilla, and looked back into the parlor toward Ophelia. He could see her there, smiling at the scene, all support for her friend. For him.

God, how he loved her even more.

His mother nudged him as Remi and Priscilla stepped back. He moved forward to do his own wave. The crowd still clapped, smiling faces greeting him. But then he heard it.

Boos. He searched the crowd and saw the frowns and glares on some of the faces. A man shouted out, "Freedom for Athawick!"

Grantham blinked at the words, which hit him like a punch. He'd seen them before, in the flyers put up all over the capital...but hearing them? That was another story. It felt so much more real. He could see the crowd stirring, confused, leaning toward the man. More than one man now, calling out the slogan over and over in a never-ending refrain.

One of the guards on the terrace turned. "I'll signal to have them removed."

Grantham shook his head. "No. These are my people. They are allowed to have a voice."

The guard looked confused and Grantham understood why. His father would have had them tarred and feathered, likely. No one would have dared to oppose him.

Grantham didn't want that. He lifted his hand one last time, hoping his feelings weren't clear on his face, and then stepped back into the antechamber, the family following. His mother closed the terrace doors hurriedly, but the boos and hollers were still heard, even from the distance. Grantham stopped in the middle of the room, staring straight ahead but seeing nothing.

"Grantham," Sasha said, stepping toward him.

He held up a hand. "No. Please. No." He faced the guard who had spoken to him on the terrace and followed the family back inside. "Be sure the crowd disperses safely, but I want to make it clear that those who speak in protest against me are not to be harassed or harmed."

The guard's brow wrinkled and Grantham could see he wished to argue, but he did not. He only inclined his head. "Yes, Your Majesty. I'll go down and spread the word amongst the division."

He hustled from the room and Grantham let out a ragged sigh. His gaze flitted to Ophelia and their eyes met. He felt her support, her understanding, her sadness on his behalf and it was too much. He shook his head and strode from the room, away from her, away from the family, away from the still buzzing crowd below...away from everything but his duty and his failure, because those were the albatross he wore around his neck at all times.

~

Ophelia didn't care how it looked to the others. When Grantham speared her with that gaze that was so broken, so devastated, so uncertain and then fled the room, she didn't wait or ask permission. She followed him, racing behind him down the hallways. He didn't go to his study, as she expected, but past it and into a parlor where she had never been before.

She entered the room and stopped. The furniture was all cleared away in here, save a settee placed against a far wall. There were fencing tools and dummies she assumed were meant to practice combat in every corner. A place for a man to fight. And yet Grantham stood in the middle of the room, his head bent.

"Go away," he snapped without looking at her. "I don't want you here, Ophelia."

She heard the order, but also the deep pain behind it and she didn't move.

He pivoted, dark eyes flashing. "I said get out."

Instead, she turned and moved to shut the door. She saw Remi coming down the hallway. He stopped as he saw her. Their eyes met and held, and she made a decision. One that revealed far too much to Remi, she was certain. Far too much to herself.

She shook her head gently and shut the door.

Turning, she said nothing as she moved to Grantham. He stiffened as she touched his upper arm, and he felt so fragile in that moment. So breakable in his despair. But he was still fighting. Fighting her, fighting the future, fighting the pain and the fear.

"I said I don't want you," he whispered, his voice breaking. "I want to see Remi."

"And you will," she said. She reached for him, touching his cheek, then sliding her hand to the back of his head. Gently she guided him down until his forehead rested on her shoulder. Only then did she feel the fight go out of him. He slumped, his shoulders rolling forward, his breath becoming ragged. She wrapped her arms around him and held him through it, demanding nothing, saying nothing.

She was what he needed. She knew it in her soul. And she wasn't going to be anything less than that right now. She drew him to the settee and they sat. He rested his head against her arm, and together they simply breathed.

Finally, he lifted his head and shook it. "I was raised never to let this kingdom fail," he said.

She took his hands and rested them in her lap, cradling them between her own. "You aren't."

He shrugged. "That is uncertain. You see how far this rebellion has come. They are willing to come onto palace grounds and scream for my removal and their freedom. They were willing to follow our family to London and physically threaten and harm my sisters. This isn't some disorganized group of two or three who are drunkenly screeching in a pub. This is…this is real desire for self-governance. A *real* request for the end of sovereign rule."

She pursed her lips, focused entirely on him. And not just what he said and the tone he said it with. She saw every flicker in his stare, felt every nuance of his body language.

"Do you fear they're…they're in the right?" she asked.

He stiffened, and that was her answer. Written in brilliant color all over his handsome face before he sighed. "I don't know. I have studied the representative governments that have grown up in the past few years. There is no doubt that there is merit to the idea."

"Then…" She drew a deep breath because she knew full well she was overstepping. "Grantham, is there a way that you could do as they wished?"

He flinched slightly. "Surrender the throne, you mean? Destroy what my family has heralded and protected for centuries?"

She touched his cheek again. "I know you, Grantham. What you wish to herald and protect are your people. Perhaps your legacy is to do that in the best way possible to help them find success without the violence we saw when the colonies rebelled against English rule."

He let out a shaky breath. "This country is so small. A war would devastate everyone who lives here and leave us open to invasion from those who wish to control the power our location provides."

"I can't tell you what to do," she said softly. "This is not my country, nor my people. But I hate to see you paint the future with only one brush. With only what your father browbeat into you as the reference. You deserve better. And so do those you reign over."

He sighed heavily before he cupped her cheeks. He leaned in and she breathed him in before he kissed her gently. "I value your opinion. And I will think about it."

She watched as he rose and moved toward the door. She followed, smoothing her skirts. "I'm sure Remi is pacing the hallway, waiting for you."

He nodded. "And I must speak to him. But…thank you."

She opened the door and found Remi leaning against the wall. He straightened up and looked at her, searching her face for answers. Then he looked past her at his brother. His expression was a combination of understanding and worry. At least Grantham had support.

She slipped away with one last glance, but Grantham wasn't looking at her, but at his brother as they spoke quietly. The king was back, focused on his duties. That was how it had to be, but oh, how she regretted the loss of the man who needed and relied on her.

Grantham met Remi's eyes as Ophelia walked away and immediately went on edge. There was something to the way his brother walked, to the spark in his stare that let Grantham know something had happened.

"What is it?" he asked softly.

Remi pursed his lips. "A runner arrived just after you left us, sent ahead by Jonah and Ilaria. They are returning, arriving tomorrow, and they are not alone."

Grantham rubbed a hand over his eyes. "And that's all that was said. No missive of explanation or preparation?"

"I was confused by that, as well. But this must mean they've found the leader of the rebellion. Who else could be coming?"

"It seems so," Grantham said softly. His heart throbbed at the thought. "I will finally face off with the man who wants me gone."

"And how do you feel about that?" Remi asked.

"A king doesn't feel—"

"I'm not asking about the king's feelings, I'm asking about my brother's." Remi interrupted. "They are not the same."

"They are still the same, at least for now," Grantham said, bending his head. "But that isn't a way to dodge your question. I am…I'm uncertain how I feel. Since I don't know who this man is, what his motivations are, it's hard for me to picture how it will go. And I'm uncomfortable about that, I admit. But I suppose we will know tomorrow. Odd that we received Jonah's letter this morning saying they were still looking and this less detailed message this afternoon that they are on their way."

"The first must have been delayed," Remi said, and then he sighed. "What can I do? And if you say nothing I will punch you with far more force than I did this morning when we sparred."

"I would hope so," Grantham grunted. "Since you hardly touched me this morning."

Remi rolled his eyes as Grantham pondered his brother. Since becoming king, Grantham had tried to manage everything on his own. But this…this was too much. Ophelia had helped him see it, had helped him realize that he could accept help and not be weak.

"You have always had a closer bond to our people," he said with a sigh.

Remi looked confused. "I…suppose that might be true. In my

position I was allowed to be freer, or I decided to be, the consequences be damned."

Grantham nodded. "I do need your help. Meet with Dash. Together, I need you to find a way to uncover how many of them want…" He hesitated because he could scarcely say it. "How many of them want me gone."

Remi's eyes went wide. "Wait, are you considering abdication? And…what? Leave me in charge? I'm certainly not equipped or interested in—"

"I wouldn't drop this burden on anyone in this family," Grantham interrupted. "I'm not considering abdication, Remi. These people, they don't want a king or a queen. Not me, not you, not either of our sisters."

"You would consider that option," Remi whispered. "Self-rule. What do they call it? Democracy."

"If the sentiment is popular, I think I must. My duty is first to the people."

Remi stared at him for a very long time, long enough that Grantham started to worry he had broken his brother. Then Remi smiled slightly. "Father is rolling in his grave right now."

Grantham barked out a laugh, despite the difficult circumstance. "Well, that is a happy side benefit to this position we find ourselves in."

Remi grinned at him. "I almost wish I could see it."

"As for this meeting with the person Ilaria and Jonah are bringing tomorrow, I also hope you'll be available to join me for it. I'll need your powers of observation to help me determine what is truth and what is something else."

"I will be with you to the end, Grantham," Remi promised. "Whatever that end may be." He turned to the door. "I'll go to Dash right now. We'll work this out."

As his brother left, Grantham sagged. He had been fighting a war for a long time. Since even before his father's death. Fighting to find out who he was, fighting to be a better king than the last man who had held the crown. But now, for the first time, he felt a flare of hope.

He just prayed he wasn't foolish to believe that something could change. That this decision could be better for his country, rather than labeling him the man who had destroyed his home, his family and the life of his people.

CHAPTER 19

It had been hours since the situation on the terrace and her encounter with Grantham in the parlor. Now Ophelia sat on the terrace with the queen, Priscilla and Sasha, watching them huddle together, trying to work out the future.

She was an outsider to the conversation. Priscilla had been enveloped in their fold, but Ophelia had no place. She was Grantham's lover, nothing more, and she doubted anyone outside of Priscilla had guessed that shocking fact.

In a way, Grantham was an outsider, too. Oh, he shared the same royal blood, the same troubled past. But he had to be outside because of his duty.

The doors to the palace opened, and Remi and Thomas stepped out. Ophelia could see their smiles were forced as they crossed to the ladies.

"We still have time before supper and sunset," Remi said as he leaned down to kiss Priscilla's cheek. "Thomas and I thought we might persuade you ladies to take a walk in the gardens. Shake off a bit of this gloom."

Sasha and Priscilla stood together. Sasha linked her arm through her husband's. "A fine idea. Mama, Ophelia, will you join us?"

Ophelia glanced back at the house. Grantham wasn't coming. He was likely holed up in his study, trying to work out what to do. How to do it. How to not fail, as was his greatest fear.

"Ophelia?" Priscilla said.

She shook off her thoughts. "Not tonight, perhaps. I'm a little tired—I may take my rest."

"I will also stay here," the queen said with a smile for the foursome. "You enjoy yourselves."

The others exchanged a look, but then off they went, down the terrace steps into the garden below. For a short time, their voices could be heard, talking and laughing, though perhaps in a more subdued way than they might have before the presentation earlier in the day.

The queen turned to Ophelia with a smile. "It is good to see them all so happy."

Ophelia nodded. "I can imagine. All your children have been very lucky in their marriages, it seems. All but Grantham—er, the king."

Queen Giabella's gaze flitted over her, seeing too much as she leaned back in her chair. "I fear I allowed my husband too much control over how Grantham was raised and treated. But I think he has told you as much."

Ophelia dropped her gaze. "It may have come up that the previous king was not always…kind."

"And you are, for putting it so diplomatically. A fine quality in a potential match for a king."

Ophelia drew back. "I'm not certain I could be considered that, Your Majesty."

Giabella arched a brow. "Do not play chess with a queen, my dear. We are put on the board to win." She leaned forward. "Are you in love with my son?"

Ophelia was so taken aback by the direct question that she nearly fell from her seat. She gripped the edge, trying to stop the swaying as she processed the question.

Of course the answer was yes. There wasn't even a sliver of doubt, though she hadn't allowed herself to consider it before. She loved Grantham and she had for some time. It was why she kept reaching for him, even when he pulled away. It was why his happiness was so tantamount to her. Why she feared for his health and safety as he navigated this delicate path he had been placed upon.

The queen was still staring at her and Ophelia dropped her chin. Love him or not, it didn't change the challenges. "I want what is best for him," she said at last.

Giabella smiled slightly. "Another diplomatic answer. And one I cannot fault. I think he deserves someone who wants the best for him. After all, he thinks of what is best for everyone else in his orbit. If I could choose a match for him, it would be someone who could understand the weight he bears and offer to carry it in small but important ways."

For a moment they were quiet together, staring off toward the garden as the sun began to dip into the horizon of the sea beyond. The queen did not seem to require a response to her suggestion. Ophelia wasn't certain she had one.

The door behind them opened and she turned, heart leaping, but it was not Grantham there, but Dashiell Talbot instead. She glanced toward the queen and saw the light in her gaze, the burst of happiness to see this man.

"Your Majesty, Lady Ophelia," he began. "I'm sorry to interrupt."

"Not at all, Dashiell," Queen Giabella said, rising and moving toward him, almost as if she were drawn to do so. Ophelia saw how Dash tracked her. "Was there something you needed?"

He inclined his head. "The celebration of lights."

Giabella sucked in a breath and shook her head. "Of course. I forgot the time."

"It has been a trying day," he said softly. "And why I'm here to remind you."

Giabella smiled before she returned her attention to Ophelia. "Our annual advent celebration involves a beautiful procession of lights. The preparations begin this time of year and I have some items to sign off on. You understand."

"Of course," Ophelia said, rising. "Don't concern yourself with me."

"Dash," Giabella said.

The secretary moved toward her and then stopped. Ophelia noticed how he flexed his hand at his side, as if he wanted to touch the queen, but could not. Instead he motioned for her to lead and followed behind a step as they entered the house.

Ophelia sighed. The connection between the pair was palpable, and yet there were boundaries that seemed impossible to cross. Which felt all too familiar. She smoothed her skirts and was about to enter the house herself, retire to her room to think, when the door opened yet again and this time it was who she had been waiting for all along. Grantham exited, and when he saw her moving toward him, they both stopped.

He shifted, his expression hardening, and she braced herself. He might wish to chastise her for how she had interfered with his conversation with his brother earlier and she readied herself for that.

"Ophelia, I-I—" He stopped himself and shook his head. Then he shocked her by closing the rest of the distance between them. He caught her upper arms and pressed his forehead to hers. She gasped, wrapping her arms around his waist as they held each other for a breath, two.

"Things will change soon," he said softly. "I'll have to..." He pulled back and stared down into her eyes. "Ophelia, I would not drag you into my chaos."

She shook her head. "I like chaos, Grantham."

He laughed, though the sound was hollow. Then his smile fell. "Jonah and Ilaria will be back tomorrow and they bring the kind of chaos no one will like. Things will shift...they'll..." His voice broke. "We may only have tonight left."

The thought sent a shiver down her spine. "Oh."

"Will you—could we—"

"Come with me," she whispered, catching his hand and drawing him toward the palace.

"Where?" he asked, though he followed her without argument.

She peeked back over her shoulder at him, this man she loved and very well might lose. "My room," she said. "I'm taking you to my room."

~

Grantham followed Ophelia into her chamber. A maid was there, stirring the fire. He stopped at the door, expecting Ophelia to blush and gasp and find a way to explain away why he was there. Instead, she arched a brow at the young woman. "That will be all, Lydia."

The maid cast him a quick glance, but curtseyed and hustled out. He stared at Ophelia. That was a queenly move. It made it so very easy to imagine her at his side, helping him run his kingdom.

If there was a kingdom left to be run.

"Will she talk?" he asked, reaching behind himself to shut the door and turning the key carefully.

She shrugged. "Perhaps. What does it matter now? Your country doesn't see it as a sin and I'm not in England."

He smiled and walked past her, looking around the chamber. It was pretty enough, not overly small. He shook his head. "You know, I'm not sure I've ever been in this room. I probably haven't been in half the rooms in the palace."

She watched him pace around. "I don't doubt it. It's a big place and you're a busy man. Why would you come into every corner?"

He pivoted to look at her. "Had I been aware of every corner, perhaps all these dramatics with my people could have been avoided."

She moved toward him. "Or maybe they couldn't have. Don't torture yourself with what could have been. There is enough to torment yourself about in the present without dragging all the what-ifs of the past into it."

"You are very wise," he said, and loved how the corners of her lips twitched at his teasing.

"Perhaps I've an old soul," she said. "But we both know this witty repartee is not why we came here."

"No?" he asked.

She took his hand and pulled him closer. "No." She touched his face. "If you are right and this might be the last night we can do this...we shouldn't waste it. Especially since we'll be expected for supper in a few short hours."

"Oh no, I'm not going to supper," he said softly. "I'm not wasting one moment of whatever time we have left for something so frivolous as food."

She cupped the back of his neck and drew him down. Just before she touched her lips to his, she whispered, "Good."

He groaned against her mouth, reveling in the gentle pressure of her lips as it transformed to something hungrier. She pulled away and pointed toward the bed.

"Undress," she ordered, and walked away.

He chuckled as he watched her go to the door and lock it. "You know, I'm the one in charge around here."

"Are you?" She leaned against the door and watched as he removed his clothing piece by piece, laying them out against the back of the closest chair.

"For now," he corrected and couldn't find humor in the statement.

She moved toward him. "No thoughts of that right now. Not here." She reached him and slid her hands up his bare chest, across his shoulders. "Don't be anything but mine tonight."

He shivered at that idea. Hers. Tonight, tomorrow, forever. None of it would ever be enough. But beggars, unfortunately, could not be choosers and he would take what he could get until there was nothing else left and she was gone.

He caught her waist, pulling her against him. "I'm yours," he whispered, as close to the declaration of love that would be so unfair to both of them. He kissed her before she could ask for more, and she lifted against his naked body with another of those pretty little gasps she sometimes made when he touched her.

They were music to his ears.

She pulled away. "Lie down, please. On your stomach."

He wrinkled his brow. "I may not be the very best at this...but I'm fairly certain that we won't get where we want to go if I'm on my stomach."

"Your Majesty, please," she huffed, playfully frustrated. "Now."

He rolled his eyes, participating in their game, as usual. It was entirely a game now, though perhaps it always had been. He got onto her bed and lay on his stomach, propping his head on his forearms.

He heard her rustling behind him and glanced over to find she had stripped open the buttons along the front of her gown and undressed down to her chemise. He stared at the expanse of bare legs and gorgeous curves presented before him, and reached out a hand.

Which she promptly swatted away gently. "Honestly, you are out of control," she laughed. "Let me just do this."

"What is *this*?" he demanded, although he rested his head back down.

He felt the bed shift beneath her weight. She moved next to him and then he felt her hands against his skin. She massaged the tense muscles of his shoulders, then down his back, slowly and firmly releasing some of the tension he'd been carrying all day.

All day? No, all week, all month, all year...all his life.

He groaned into the pillows. "Good God, Ophelia."

Laughter laced her tone as she said, "I'll take that as an affirmation to keep going."

"Never stop. This is how I want to die."

Her hands hesitated. "Don't tease about that. Anything else, not that. I'm not so foolish as to be blind to the fact that you're in danger."

He pursed his lips. She wasn't wrong. No matter what he did going forward, there would be very angry people left in his wake. Someone had already tried to hurt his sisters as a way to get to him. He knew full well that he was a much higher value target.

"You're worried about me," he said softly.

Her hands faltered. "Of course."

"Even though you find me entirely irritating."

"Well…not entirely," she conceded. "Not anymore. What about you? Do you still think I'm an outrageous hoyden?"

He rolled onto his back and stared up at her. "Oh yes," he whispered. "It's one of your most charming qualities."

They held each other's stares for a beat, two. She said nothing, but slung her leg over his body, straddling his hips. She tugged the chemise away in one smooth motion before she leaned over him, finding his mouth with hunger and desire and, yes, desperation. Somehow the fact that she felt it as much as he did was comforting. He wouldn't suffer alone, at least.

But he couldn't think of that now. He could only think of how sweet she tasted, how perfectly she fit against him, how her nails raked against his skin and her hips rocked against his.

It took nothing to get hard for her. She didn't even have to touch him, in truth. But she was touching him and he was on fire. He cupped her hips, digging his fingers into the softness of her, loving how she gasped against his mouth and kept grinding against him.

He reached between them, stroking her, finding her already wet, already hot and ready. He took himself in hand, aching from the anticipation, aching more when she shifted and together they aligned their bodies.

She dropped down over him, taking him inside in one deep stroke. They gasped together as he sat up. She began to ride him while he cradled her in his arms, their kisses growing ever more heated as the pleasure mounted between them. He felt her began to shift, finding the rhythm that would bring her what she needed. He pulled away from her mouth so he could watch her as she used him. Watched the way her cheeks flushed, the way her head tilted back as she arched and moaned in more earnest.

The ripples began, her pussy milking him as she began to come. He lifted into her from below, still watching as she came, marking every twitch of her face and harsh gasp of her breath. Her thrusts got more erratic as her nails dug into his skin, marking him in a way he wished was permanent so he would see the scars and know this had been real.

Her wild and explosive orgasm didn't only please her. Every shuddering thrust sent lightning bolts of pleasure through his cock, across every nerve ending of his body. The need to come increased and he had to fight with it, to let her have every drop of pleasure. Only when he felt her go limp, the gripping heat of her fading a fraction, did he roll her to her back.

She lifted into him, seeking all over again as he took her. And it was a taking, a claiming that he could never say out loud. He took her and marked her and made her his before he could take no more and withdrew to come between them.

He collapsed next to her, gathering her close, their panting breaths and pounding heartbeats matching in the quiet of the chamber. For what felt like a blissful lifetime, they simply lay like that. But reality had to return, didn't it?

He sighed. "I ought to get up, go back to it."

She tilted her head. "I thought you weren't going to let something so frivolous as food keep you from me and everything we are going to do tonight."

"Perhaps not food, but duty," he said.

She reached up to touch his face. "Send word that you are here if there is an emergency, and then stay with me."

He blinked. "Tell Dash that I'm with you?"

She swallowed. "Mr. Talbot is who you would tell?"

"Until this situation with the courtiers is resolved, he's helping me," Grantham said.

"Well, I don't care if he knows. Or if anyone else knows." She shifted up to her elbow. "Please stay with me."

He lifted a hand to trace her jawline, her cheek, to slide his fingers into her silky hair and feel it loosen from the style and begin to tangle around him. He didn't answer her plea, but simply pressed his mouth back to hers, shifting her onto the pillows to cover her once more.

The breakfast room was empty when Ophelia entered it the next morning. She was not rested, but she was entirely satisfied after a long night in Grantham's arms. They'd made love over and over, but they'd also talked. Not about the situation with his kingdom, but about music and books, life and dreams. If she had loved him before, that emotion was now richer and deeper, multiplied every day they spent time together.

"And still hopeless," she muttered as she grabbed a plate at the sideboard and began looking through the food on offer. Before she could take too much, Dashiell Talbot entered the room. He looked very official and serious, though he cast her a quick smile before taking a plate.

"Good morning, my lady," he said.

"Good morning," she replied. "I must say I'm not sad to see another person. I wondered if I had stumbled upon some official food I wasn't meant to touch."

"Touch away," he encouraged. "The kippers are especially good."

"Excellent." Ophelia took one of the slabs of fish and added it to her plate. "You aren't getting any, though?"

He smiled. "It is a favorite of mine but not of the queen, and it is for her that I am making this plate." He placed a few items here or there.

"She isn't coming down?" Ophelia asked.

Talbot's expression wavered slightly. "She must prepare to meet with the others. Princess Ilaria and Count Crawford returned to the palace just a short time ago."

Ophelia nearly dropped her plate. "They've returned? And I assume they have the leader of his uprising group with them?"

Talbot turned to face her fully, his expression lined with surprise. "You know a great deal, my lady."

She held his stare for a moment and saw in it a true reflection of her own worries and fears for Grantham. She set her plate on the sideboard and folded her arms before herself. "When you care for someone in the position that the king is in...or the queen...well, you know," she said softly.

Talbot's cheek twitched and he turned his face, almost like those words were a slap. Then he cleared his throat and forced himself to look at her again. "You must understand, Lady Ophelia, that this is not an easy road. There are complications."

"I suppose you would understand that better than most."

He inclined his head. "If you will excuse me, I must deliver this to Gia—to Queen Giabella so she may eat something before she joins the meeting shortly. I hope you will not be upset to eat alone."

"Of course not," Ophelia said, and waved him toward the door. "Good day, Mr. Talbot."

He strode out and she sighed as she picked up her plate. Now that she knew the man who threatened Grantham's position... perhaps his very life...was in the palace, she wished she hadn't taken so much food. She couldn't eat it, she knew that.

Still, she sat and tried, picking through the offerings as best she could. But all the while, her thoughts raced. Grantham would meet with his sister, brother-in-law and this man first. He'd told her so last night when they'd briefly broached the topic. Any time it came up, she saw the lines of worry and grief on his face.

Did he have them there now? Would he come out safe or broken?

She pushed from the table with a screech of chair leg against wood floor. With an apologetic look for the footman standing by to take her plate, she slipped from the room. In the hallway, she looked in the direction she'd have to go to enter Grantham's study.

But no, she had no place there. He was her lover and that was temporary. She could be there for him after these trying hours were finished, but she couldn't barge into a room where she hadn't been invited and demand a place at his table.

She worried her hands and moved down the hallway in the opposite direction to his study. She entered a parlor that connected to the terrace and stepped outside.

It was a sunny day but cool, and she breathed in the crisp air as she stepped to the edge of the terrace and looked down over the garden. Some of the last autumn flowers were blooming and their brightness warmed her heart in these dark times.

She straightened up. The same blooms might also warm Grantham. She would pick him a bouquet and deliver it to his chamber to be waiting for him. A reminder that she was thinking of him and that there was color even in the darkest times.

That resolved, she smiled as she all but skipped down the stairs and moved toward the flowerbeds. No one else was in the garden. Probably best since she intended to do this without asking permission. She could apologize later if she wasn't meant to pick flowers in the royal garden.

She began to choose blooms, picking carefully so they were the best and brightest of the fading bunch. She had a handful of the prettiest ones and was searching through even more when she heard a sound behind her.

She pivoted to face it and nearly staggered into the flowerbed in shock. There, not three feet away from her, was Stephen Blairford,

Grantham's disgraced courtier. His cheeks were slashed with stubble, his clothing far more casual than she'd seen him wear in the palace. But it was his expression that made her drop her hands, flowers scattering across the lawn at her feet.

He looked wild. His eyes were bright with emotion, his face lined with hatred as he stared at her.

"What are you doing here?" she asked softly, glad she could meter her emotions when terror gripped her.

He tilted his head. "Why, I've come to collect *you*, my dear lady."

She glanced back up toward the palace. "Me? Why would you want me?"

"Because His Majesty is due to lose something important to him. And I think you might just be that." She started to turn away, but Blairford pulled out a pistol from his pocket and leveled it on her. "Tsk, tsk, Lady Ophelia. Don't be a fool. Now let's go."

"They await you in your study," Dash said to Grantham as they strode down the hallway together. "You will meet with them briefly on your own and then the queen, Princess Sasha and Prince Remington will join you, as per your request."

Grantham nodded. "Very good. Thank you for arranging things in the absence of a trusted courtier to do so."

"You may always depend on me," Dash said softly.

"Yes." Grantham stopped at the door and smiled at him. "I know. And I appreciate that, and your great care in how you tend to my mother."

Something in Dash's gaze flickered, but he inclined his head. "Ring if you have any need. I won't be far."

Grantham excused him with a wave and then smoothed his coat. In that room were his sister and Jonah...but also the leader of the resistance movement against him. At last he would face off with the man who had begun this madness. The one who might end it.

He pushed the door open and entered. Ilaria and Jonah stood together before the fire and he nodded to them briefly before his gaze found the only other person in the room. Not a man, but a woman, and she met his stare without hesitation.

"Grantham," Ilaria said. "This is Marabelle Fowler. The leader of the rebellion group."

"Your Majesty," she said with the slightest of curtsies.

Grantham stared at her. "You are…unexpected."

"You thought to find a man waiting for you?" she asked with a slight smile. "Everyone does."

He glanced at Jonah and Ilaria. "I'm surprised this wasn't mentioned."

Jonah wrinkled his brow. "We wrote a letter explaining it."

Grantham shook his head. "I only received a message from a courier saying you were on your way. No mention of any other details." Jonah and Ilaria appeared confused, but Grantham pushed questions aside. "Not that it matters. Man or woman, you and I have a great deal to discuss, Miss Fowler."

"More than you know," she said. "But I assume the others are to join us soon."

"The rest of the family," Grantham said softly. "The family you wish to destroy."

Ilaria stepped forward. "Grantham, it…it may be more complicated than that. I wish you had received our earlier missive. I explained some of what was told to us."

Grantham shook his head, but before he could say anything further, the door to the parlor opened and the rest of the family streamed in. His mother first, and Miss Fowler flinched ever so slightly. Remi and Sasha came after.

They all stared at their guest with as much surprise as Grantham had felt. He sighed. "Yes, this is she. Marabelle Fowler is her name."

"None of the spouses?" Miss Fowler said.

Remi arched a brow. "This is a royal matter first. Who are you?"

"*That* is the material question," the young woman said, and her eyes drifted back to Queen Giabella. Softened with what almost looked like regret. "Since Princess Ilaria's message didn't reach you, I fear what I'm about to tell you will be a shock."

Giabella shifted slightly. "There have been a great many shocks as of late. I assure you, we can bear it."

There was a flutter of a sad smile across the young woman's face. Almost a grimace, as if she was causing herself pain. "Let me tell you about my mother."

Grantham stepped toward her. "This is folly. You have come here to treat with the king, have you not? Then why don't we start the negotiation rather than drag it out with all this nonsense."

She didn't back away from him. She showed no fear. And her bright blue eyes held his without wavering. "My mother's name was Violet Croix."

The queen made a soft sound in her throat and staggered back. Jonah stepped to her, holding her elbow gently to steady her. For half a second, not even a heartbeat, Grantham didn't understand why that name would cause such a reaction in his mother.

And then he recalled it. "My father's...my father's mistress," he whispered.

"One of them," she said. "I'm sorry, Your Majesty." She directed that toward the queen, who was still staring. "She was one of the mistresses your father placed in the palace. *Our* father."

Once, when he was fifteen, Grantham had fallen out of a rowboat he and Remi had taken out to sea. He'd heard his brother shouting from above the water, but it was all muted and echoing until he'd been pulled to safety by Dash, who had followed them to the beach, suspecting they were up to no good.

This moment reminded him of that one. The others were talking, but he was under the sea. Cut off from everything in his shock. He looked across the room to his mother and found the queen also silent, her face entirely pale and her hands shaking as she gripped Jonah's arm.

He shook his head and brought himself back to the surface. To reality.

"—cannot be possible," Sasha was saying. "It was only fifteen years ago that his mistress lived here! You are in your twenties, I would wager."

"He kept more than one woman under this roof over the years," Giabella interrupted softly, her cheeks flaming with embarrassment and pain. "Under my nose." She tilted her head. "Look at her eyes."

Giabella released Jonah and began to cross the room. She stopped a foot from Miss Fowler. Her bottom lip trembled. "Look at her eyes," she repeated. "And then look at Remi's."

Grantham did so. Remi was the only one who had inherited their father's bright blue stare. And the queen was right, Marabelle's was the same. Her nose was like Ilaria's. As was the way she tilted her head just slightly.

He shut his eyes a moment, and when he opened them he pushed back his shoulders. He had to be king, not brother, not son. King took precedence.

"Let us assume for a moment that I believe you," he said softly. "That you are the illegitimate child of King Alistair. Is *this* why you're doing all this? Out of some fit of pique?"

"No," Miss Fowler breathed. "Not at all. When my mother became with child, she was pushed from this house and foisted onto a man who married her and raised me as his own…reluctantly. He made it abundantly clear who I was and what I was. That I was not wanted by him because I was the king's bastard. That I was not wanted by the king, either. When I got old enough, I began to research the monarchy. I was obsessed."

Grantham pursed his lips. "Obsessed enough to want to destroy it."

"Obsessed enough to realize it *should* be destroyed," she corrected in a surprisingly gentle tone. "This monarchy is rotten to its core, Your Majesty. Yes, we are a more progressive society than many. Yes, there are good things about what your family has done over the centuries of power. But there are also terrible things."

Grantham shifted. "Yes. I won't deny that. I cannot."

"Nor will *I* deny that you are a good man on the whole. There has been nothing to be found that says you are anything like your father. Like many of your worst grandfathers before you." She held his stare. "But there are no good kings, sir. Only tolerable ones. Power at this level, it corrupts. It must in order to believe that it should hold sway over those beneath it. So yes, I believe that this monarchy should fall and the rule of the people should rise in its place, as it has in many other nations."

He turned away, pacing to his desk and leaning against it with both hands. She was saying out loud the things he had thought himself many times. Things he had feared.

"I'm sorry," Marabelle said. Grantham turned back toward her and saw that she was speaking to Giabella. "You and my mother were both victims of the last king. I am truly not trying to hurt you."

Remi stepped forward, his cheeks bright with color. "How can you say that when you tried to kill my sisters in London? Your...*your* sisters."

Marabelle's mouth dropped open and she stared first at her accuser and then at Grantham. She looked truly shocked at the accusation. "No. *No*, I never did that."

"Of course you did," Jonah said, moving to stand with Ilaria. "The attack on my wife and later on Sasha was played out by members of *your* group. They claimed it, they left your flag."

Marabelle looked truly confused and upset by the accusation. "Why didn't you confront me with this lie earlier?"

Ilaria tilted her head. "Because we wanted you to come with us."

Marabelle sighed. "I see." She pivoted toward Grantham. "My group *has* made its moves, Your Majesty. We protested at the presentation of Prince Remington and Princess Priscilla. We have posted flyers and gathered support from those on our side. We have walked away from the unfair treatment by your counts. But I swear to you, on my life, that I never made any moves to harm the princesses." She glanced at Ilaria. "You and I have spent two days in a carriage. Please tell me you believe me."

Ilaria looked at her and then to Grantham. "I…I would have a hard time believing it. Miss Fowler seemed honest in all she told us. And never unhinged or violent."

Grantham ran a hand through his hair as he exchanged a look with Remi. "If not you, perhaps someone else in your group. Someone with more extreme methods."

Marabelle swallowed, pacing the room. "I don't believe so. And if they were violating the tenets of what our group believed, they would also have to be connected to the palace."

"What do you mean?"

"The attacks happened in London, yes? I don't know of anyone bound to us who went away during that time. We were all working on our message to you for when you returned. The one you didn't respond to."

Grantham stared at her. "What message?"

"We reached out with requests," she said. "Weeks ago. And your response back made it clear you did not care for what we demanded."

"I don't know what you're talking about," he said. "I never saw demands."

"The letter returned was signed by you." She pulled a folded paper from her pocket and handed it to him.

He stared because the hand was, indeed, almost identical to his own. The signature even more like his. But he hadn't written this message, he was certain of it.

He was about to ask more questions when the door opened and Dash entered the room. Giabella took a step toward him before she stopped herself.

"Dash, what is it?" Grantham asked, his ears still ringing from all these shocks.

"I'm sorry to intrude, but we've just received a message about

Lady Ophelia." Dash sounded…panicked. The man never sounded that way, and Grantham's heart began to throb out of control as he rushed toward him.

"In regards to what?"

"She's been taken, Your Majesty, by members of *this* woman's group."

CHAPTER 21

Grantham pivoted on Marabelle, all sense of balance lost in the wake of such terrible news. "Where is she?"

"I don't know what you're talking about," she said, pulling at her arms as Jonah grabbed for them to hold her in place. "I have no idea who Lady Ophelia even is!"

"That is fucking rubbish," Remi snapped. "I'm sorry, Mama."

The queen inclined her head. "I have heard the word."

"If you've been studying, one must also assume you've been spying," said Grantham. Marabelle flinched slightly and Grantham knew he had hit a mark. "And if you knew Ophelia was important to me, she would be the perfect new target for you."

"I haven't had targets before," Marabelle snapped. "For God's sake, will you listen to me? I had nothing to do with the attacks on the princesses. I had nothing to do with the kidnapping of *anyone*."

Grantham stared at her. He had always believed himself to be a good judge of character. He knew Ilaria to be. And right now his sister believed this woman. And somehow...so did he.

"Then why?" he said, holding out a hand to take the missive Dash had brought in. He glanced down and read it out loud. "*Give in to our demands or your lover's blood will be spilled.*"

He shivered as he noted the piece of cloth sewn to the paper. He had seen Ophelia in that gown earlier, watching her as she slipped down the hallways. He'd so wanted to go to her, touch her to take some of her strength before this nightmare began.

"Ophelia," he whispered, his voice cracking.

"May I?" Marabelle took the note and scanned it. "I...I think whoever wrote this also wrote the missive I brought today. Look at the *l*. And the way the *t* is crossed."

He leaned in and examined the two side by side. She was correct. Though the handwriting on the note supposedly from him did look very much like his own, those two letters had similarities in both missives.

"Someone wishes each of us to mistrust the other. To put us at war," he murmured.

"Who would benefit from such a conflict?" Giabella asked.

Grantham lifted his gaze and tightened his jaw. "Blairford," he murmured, rushing around his desk to grab his last message from the courtier from his desk. It was a list of engagements from a week ago, something Grantham had meant to discard but had been too distracted by Ophelia's presence to do so. Now he held it next to the others and there it was, in black and white. The same slant to the *l*, the same squiggled line to the *t*.

"He was manipulating this all along," he murmured.

"He arranged for the attack on Ilaria," Jonah whispered.

"And on me," Sasha added with a shiver. "But why?"

"To make me want to react violently to my own people," Grantham whispered. "Because once I did, it would set a tone, keep me from ever allowing them too much leeway. He wanted a war to make me a despot. Hated and feared, because he saw that as a way to retain power over me."

Dash nodded, his expression sick. "Blairford would certainly have the power to intercept the demands Miss Fowler said her group sent to you, being your courtier."

"And the letter from Ilaria describing the situation with Miss

Fowler," Jonah added. "He could have intercepted them even after he was gone from the palace. But with less power, he couldn't manage to get them all. He might have been interrupted in that plan and hence, he had to take Ophelia."

Dash straightened up slightly. "Just a few days ago, I sacked one of the footmen, who I realized was related to Blairford. He'd never disclosed it."

"That might have been his last hard connection," Grantham mused. "If true, Blairford could have become desperate." He ran a hand through his hair as he tried not to buckle in utter terror.

Ophelia was with this man. This man who would create such violence for power. He would kill her, that was evident.

"Your Majesty, I do have connections in your walls," Marabelle said. "One of them might have seen something. Do I have your word you will not punish them if they reveal themselves?"

"Yes," he said. "They will have commendations, in fact, if they can help me get to Ophelia."

Jonah motioned to her. "Let me help connect you with your people, Miss Fowler."

Grantham gave him a grateful smile before he turned to Dash. "I need a mount and a gun."

Giabella rushed forward and caught his hands. "Grantham, you are king of this country. You cannot rush out to face off with such a man. It is too dangerous."

He squeezed her hands. "I will not stand by helpless, Mama. I will not be manipulated any longer or controlled. I love her."

Her expression softened. "I know."

"Then you know why I can't stay here."

She nodded and cast a glance at Dash. "Will you go with him?"

"I and many others," Dash said as he moved to the door. "I swear I will protect him with my life, Gia."

"As will I," Remi said, and followed the secretary.

Sasha was on his heels. "I'll fetch Thomas, as well."

That left Ilaria and his mother in the room with Grantham. He looked at them both, these two women he adored. He drew a deep breath. "I hope you will not hate me for whatever the future holds."

"As long as it holds your happiness and what you think is best for our people, no one who matters could ever hate you," Ilaria said softly. "Now go."

He kissed her cheek and then their mother's and ran from the room, his mind turning to Ophelia and how he could save her before it was too late. Before he lost the best thing in his life.

The hideout wasn't far from the palace, an abandoned fisherman's hut that was worn and weathered from the winds coming in off the sea. Ophelia sat in the middle of the open living space, tied to a rickety chair. Blairford paced the room, checking through the shutters now and then, as if expecting the cavalry to ride up at any moment.

God, Ophelia wished that were true. That she would be saved. But she was bracing for the worst and cataloging her life as she did so.

She watched her captor as he moved to the fire. He seemed so anxious as he warmed his hands by the flames. Perhaps if she could calm her own terror, she might be able to get out of this.

"Mr. Blairford," she said softly, as gently as she could. "Do you know what I think?"

He glared at her. "What is that, my lady?"

"I think you haven't thought this through. That you have put yourself in a corner and now you desperately want to go free." She shifted forward as far as her tight bonds would allow. "And that if you thought you had a way out, you might take it. I can give you that, sir."

His brow lowered and his eyes went cold as ice. "You think I haven't *planned* this? That every move of my life hasn't been part of this chess match?"

She flinched as his voice went up a level. He didn't allow her to speak but carried on. "I started working for King Alistair on the first day of his reign. I earned that spot as his lead courtier. I did unspeakable things to gain it."

"Unspeakable?" she repeated, terror wracking her.

He nodded slightly. "It was worth it, I regret *nothing*, because that power was limitless. I used it to my full advantage, creating every opportunity to be the only one Alistair trusted. I controlled it all, my lady. I forced wedges between him and anyone who could have turned his gaze from where I wished to focus it."

Her lips parted. "I…what does that mean?"

"I made sure he broke every bond with his wife. I made certain he followed any worst impulse when it came to his children, especially his eldest. I created doubt in every other advisor, friend or family member, until there was only me and my agenda for the future of this country. I was king, my dear. *I* was king."

She caught her breath on a sob at the idea that this man had created such pain for those around him. And now he celebrated it, like it was a game he had won. "You are a monster."

"No," he snapped. "I am an opportunist—that is not the same thing. And I knew I could do the same with Grantham when he took the throne. He and his siblings despised me, and yet I was able to convince him that my long years of experience were worth something. He was harder to manage, though. It took far more effort to wedge myself between him and his family. I did it by forcing him to push them away, by making them believe he had harmed them."

"Which is why you brought Priscilla's parents to the island," Ophelia breathed.

He smiled, thin and cruel. "Grantham and Remington came to physical blows over that. A true pleasure to see."

Tears stung at her eyes. "You bastard."

"But *you* became a problem the moment I saw how he looked at you. I thought it would end when we left London, and yet there you were and he toppled at your whorish feet. Even when you intruded where you didn't belong—"

"The day I was sent to where he was holding his meetings," she whispered. "But what was the purpose of these manipulations? To overthrow the monarchy?"

He laughed. "God, no. I can control *a* person, not *the* people. I don't want anything less than the power I deserve. I heard him speak to his father about granting more power to those under them. I made sure he suffered for that idea, but I could tell he was still pondering it as he took the throne. I tried to make it unpalatable with the attacks on his family, by demanding he overthrow the movement with violence."

"To put a wedge between him and those he ruled. To erase any love they had for him." She shook her head. "But it didn't work. He outsmarted you and saw you for what you are."

His jaw clenched. "Yes. He took everything I'd built from me. And so I am going to do the same to him. I will break him now, make him and his family weak to the attacks about to come. When it is over, there will be a new puppet in place. One who will be more than happy to return me to my rightful place."

She thought of the men she had met that morning that felt like a lifetime ago now. The aristocracy of this country. She had to assume they were each in line for the throne themselves, though far along the line of succession.

"Count Hadley," she whispered.

Blairford smiled slightly. "You are intelligent, I will give you that. I should have known it would be too much for Grantham to resist. My failing. And unfortunately it shall be *your* death. Because you can never be queen. I made that mistake once already, allowing Alistair to match with Giabella. She was also too intelligent for her own good."

He stepped closer and brought out the same gun he had used to force her here earlier. Once again, he leveled it on her and she began to fight her bonds, even though she knew in her heart that it would be useless to do so. He would shoot her. He would kill her.

All to destroy Grantham. And it would work because he loved her. She knew that as surely as she knew her own heart. Tears began to run down her face as she thought of the future he would steal from them. The pain he would cause the man she adored so deeply and completely.

"Now," he said softly. "You are about to die for a cause. I hope that helps somewhat."

She forced herself to remain calm even as she stared at the barrel of that horrible gun. Blairford was right about one thing: she was intelligent. She knew that. And if she could just focus, she might be able to figure a way out of this. Or at least drag it out long enough that someone would come to help her.

And then it hit her. "Wait! What if it were a cause I, too, supported?" she asked.

He glared down at her. "You can't save yourself."

"I could save you," she offered. "Save you the trouble you will create and the comfort you will lose."

"How?" he asked. "More for my own curiosity about how you think you can save yourself."

She shifted. "Do you think I've done all this for nothing?" she asked. "Queen was my goal, Blairford, and I would do anything to get that title. Think of it. What if you had a person on the inside? Someone Grantham trusted deeply, but was working on your agenda as surely as you are?"

He seemed to ponder it a moment, but then shook his head. "No. You love him. I can see it."

"Perhaps you saw what I wished you to see. What I wished him to see." She hated herself for that lie. It tasted like poison on her tongue, but it was worth it if it saved her life. "I could fix this without you losing everything."

He stared at her, reading her, and she prayed he saw what she wished him to see. Slowly, he lowered the gun. "I'm listening."

~

Grantham tensed as they rode onto the beach and the cottage rose in the shadowy distance. He would have thought it abandoned but for the faint flicker of firelight coming from between the warped wallboards.

Marabelle's spies had said Blairford visited this place. That he had been seen coming and going from it in the days since he'd been sacked. If the former courtier was the true culprit in Ophelia's kidnapping…this could be the place where she was being kept.

They all began to swing down from their horses. Remi stepped up, placing a hand on Grantham's shoulder. He could see the worry on his younger brother's face.

"Do you think it's a trap?" Remi asked softly.

Grantham stared off at the building again. "From Marabelle?"

He glanced back at the woman. She had come down from her horse and was quietly standing alongside Dash and the handful of guards they had brought for his situation. She'd made no effort to intervene or influence who was brought along for this rescue mission. She seemed to only care that Blairford was caught.

"No," Grantham said. "I feel she's true."

"I agree," Jonah said, and motioned to the guards. It was plain to see his military training in his movements and strategy. "We'll surround and be ready to move. Be careful."

The others began to take their places as Grantham, Remi and Dash started up the beach toward the shack. Grantham so desperately wanted to run to the building, to burst in and simply save Ophelia.

He had to control himself now. For her sake.

As they reached the shack, Grantham dropped down, crawling on his stomach to the edge of the building and peering in through a crack in the paneling. Ophelia was there and his heart leapt. It was difficult to see, but she looked to be bound to a chair in the middle of the room. She moved, so she was alive. Though he couldn't tell if she was injured.

He glanced at Remi and Dash. They both nodded. They'd seen the same thing through the gap as he did. He motioned Remi toward an entrance around the back of the shack, facing away from the sea. He moved toward the front and the door there.

When they reached it, he drew a few breaths.

"Let me go first," Dash said.

Grantham shook his head. "She is too precious to me."

"And your mother is too precious to me to allow you to—"

Grantham refused to argue. Carefully he pushed the door open. It creaked as it swung wide and Ophelia glanced back over her shoulder. Her eyes went wide when she saw him and she darted her gaze toward a small door in the corner of the room that likely led to a bedroom.

"Grantham!" she said.

"Are you harmed?" he said, motioning his head toward the door. Dash began to work his way along the wall even as Grantham moved toward her. "Did he hurt you?"

"*They* didn't hurt me," she said. "I was taken by a group, part of those in the uprising." She slightly shook her head and he sucked in a breath. Clearly she was sending whatever message Blairford had insisted on. Clever girl.

"Thank God you weren't harmed by those bastards. I swear I'll make them pay," he said. "Let me untie you."

He moved toward her, but as he did, the door she'd been indicating swung open. Blairford burst out.

"Vile bitch!" he cried out as he lifted his gun and pointed it not at her, but at Grantham.

The world began to move in slow motion. Ophelia lunged toward him, but was hindered by her position on the chair. Grantham heard the gun fire, but before he could be struck he was hit by Dash, who threw him out of the way.

Remi rushed in, a legion of guards on his heels, and another gun fired. Grantham dove for Ophelia, covering her in the hopes she wouldn't be struck. The smoky smell of powder hung in the air and Grantham looked over his shoulder. Blairford was dead, hit in the chest by one of the guards who now filled the room.

Dash was slowly rising and Remi gasped. "You've been hit," he said, moving toward him.

Dash looked down and so did Grantham. Blood had begun to spot his white shirt in the middle of his forearm. "It's minor," he said, pressing a hand to slow the bleeding.

Grantham ignored the rest and refocused on Ophelia. He yanked on the ties, pulling them enough that she could wiggle out. When her arms were free, she put them around him, trembling as he freed her feet and swept her up to his chest.

"I love you," he whispered against her hair as he carried her away from the sound and the blood and the death in that room.

"I told him I'd betray you," she whimpered, her tears wetting his shirt. "I would have told him anything to see you again."

"I know," he said as he moved toward the horses down the beach. He really didn't give a damn what happened now. The guards and Jonah could handle it. He'd let Remi manage Dash since it appeared he wasn't badly hurt.

When he got back to the palace, he would be king again. But right now he just wanted to be the man who loved this woman and had nearly lost her.

He swung up on the horse, keeping her tucked into him as he turned them toward home. She clung to him, her heart wild against his body, her sobs soft as the reality of what had nearly happened seemed to hit her. He comforted her with murmurs, by smoothing his hands across her back as they rode.

By telling her he loved her over and over, and hoping that once the smoke had cleared on this nightmare, that it might actually be enough.

CHAPTER 22

Ophelia had felt the shift in Grantham after they entered the parlor. When they were alone, he had only been her lover, handing over the reins of what must happen to the others in order to protect and cradle her.

But as the family surrounded them, all talking at once, welcoming them home, reacting to the fact that Dashiell Talbot had been shot saving Grantham and everything that Blairford had confessed before his death, she'd felt Grantham being pulled from her side. Watched him become king as he settled her onto a settee, kissed her forehead and slipped away without a word to handle what would come next.

So now she sat on that same settee, shifting between staring at the marks on her wrists where she had been bound and watching the queen pace as the royal physician tended to Dash in some other room. If Ophelia had not realized the two were in love, she certainly saw it now on every line of fear on the other woman's face.

She knew them so well, after all.

Sasha and Thomas were with the queen, as well as Jonah and Ilaria. Her children trying to offer comfort as the minutes dragged on. Priscilla was standing away from them, watching Ophelia instead of the royal family. When Ophelia dared to meet her gaze, her friend crossed to her.

"Tell me," she said, sitting beside Ophelia and drawing her head into her shoulder. Her friend smoothed her hand over her hair.

Ophelia sighed. "I thought that man would kill me. He would have. And he would have killed Grantham and the rest, out of some desperate grab for power that was slipping through his fingers."

Priscilla shivered. "I'm so glad it didn't work."

"So am I," Ophelia whispered. "Though I have no idea where that leaves me. Leaves us. There is so much to resolve."

Priscilla nodded. "And yet you have been granted such a chance, Ophelia. You stared death in the face and you lived. Did it not show you the path? The truth about your heart?"

Ophelia stared into the fire across the room. "I already knew my heart. I love Grantham and he loves me. It does not guarantee that there will be a future any more than it did before I was taken in the garden."

Priscilla took her hand. "I have known you nearly all my life. And you are a fighter for those in need, for those who deserve to be protected. If you do not fight just as hard for yourself, I shall be very cross with you."

Ophelia smiled despite the trying night. A smile that fell as Remi and Grantham entered the room. Grantham immediately crossed to his mother as Priscilla got up to go to her husband.

"He is fine. A minor injury. You may go to—"

He didn't get to finish. The queen said nothing, but simply rushed from the room. Grantham sighed before he turned his attention to Ophelia. Their eyes met and she couldn't help how hers filled with tears. He cleared his throat.

"I would like the room," he said softly, but firmly. It was not a tone that brooked refusal. Not that anyone seemed in a mood to refuse. Slowly, the others filtered out. Remi and Priscilla were last.

Both of them touched Grantham's arm before they left and closed the door behind them.

He moved to the settee and sank down beside Ophelia, sliding his knuckles across her cheek. She leaned into his hand, choking out a breath. "I thought I'd never feel your touch again."

He nodded. "I feared the same. My God, Ophelia." He leaned forward until their foreheads touched and they sat like that for a moment.

She finally cleared her throat. "Grantham, he manipulated your father. He told me he put the wedges between you and him. Between him and your mother."

Grantham's cheek twitched. "I would wager he did, now that his entire plan is becoming clearer. But my father allowed it all. He didn't care enough not to let Blairford carry out his machinations."

She nodded slowly. "But you did."

"Yes, and it almost got you killed," he said, running a hand through his hair. "Who I am, what I am, what must happen next almost ripped you from me."

She wrinkled her brow. "What must happen next?"

"My people are speaking," he said softly. "I must listen. This country will change and I fear it will not be easy. Men like Hadley, men who have benefited from the system of power like Blairford did…they will fight change. And it could get ugly. It will."

She cupped his cheeks. "But you will get through it."

He smiled at her. "When you say it, I almost believe it." He sighed and the smile faltered. "What I said to you on the beach…I meant it. I love you."

She shivered at how beautiful that was every time she heard it. "I know you do. But do you know that I love you in return? Because I do love you, Grantham. With all my heart, all my soul. All my life and my future. I love you."

She saw the absolute joy on his face at that declaration. The relief and the hope. But then he did what he had been trained to do his whole life. He pushed it down. It left his face and he became impassive.

"But love might not be enough, Ophelia. I cannot offer you peace. I don't know how long it will take to get there, if I ever will. This situation may drag out for years, with intermittent violence. I won't get to focus only on you and your happiness. I am still king—these are still my people, no matter what. I must put all my efforts into keeping this country intact, even if the monarchy cannot stand."

She straightened up and tilted her head. "Do I strike you as the kind of woman who runs away from a fight, Your Majesty?"

He smiled again. "Very much not. But this is a terrible fight, Ophelia."

"All the more reason not to face it alone," she said. "Grantham, no one in the world can offer peace. Yes, your situation is certainly more fraught than the average gentleman's, but no one could look me in the face and tell me I would never face hardship if I married them. If I loved them." She cupped his cheeks gently. "My peace, my love, is *you*. I want your peace to be me. The rest...the rest will work out."

He stared at her. "Are you truly saying you would wish to be with me?"

"Every day, in every way, until the moment I take my last breath," she said, and meant it.

He leaned in and his lips touched hers, at first feather-light and then harder and with more passion and desperation after everything they had endured.

"You know there is one wonderful thing about giving up the throne," he said between kisses.

She leaned back. "And what is that?"

"I can marry who I please. No need for political matches," he said. "And I adore you so completely. If you would be mine, I would be the luckiest man in the world."

"Lucky together," she corrected as joy overcame her. "For the rest of our lives. So if you are asking me to marry you, the answer is yes."

He laughed as he took her mouth again, and she sank into the warmth and wonder of him. And she knew she would never have to give it or him up again.

EPILOGUE

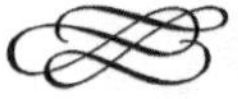

Three months later

The wedding had been held quickly and quietly, the moment the Duke and Duchess of Gilmore had been able to return to Athawick to joyfully give Ophelia away. In the time since they wed, Grantham had never once taken his queen for granted. Ophelia had stood by him through the difficult times and the joyful ones. She brought that light that burned within her into what were sometimes very dark times.

And now, as they stood together on the terrace attached to their chamber, overlooking the sun as it drifted over the cold winter sea in the distance, he held her closer.

"I have news," he said.

She turned more fully into him, her arms tightening around his waist. "I wondered when you would tell me about Remi's report on the desires of your...our people."

He glanced down at her. "How did you know Remi was ready to report... Ah...Priscilla."

"It is your own fault, two brothers marrying two best friends."

"I suppose it was badly done in a few respects, though the good far outweighs the bad, I assure you," he teased.

She laughed and it was music. Then she smoothed her hands along his spine. "Tell me."

"There does seem to be a majority who do not wish to continue under a monarchy. Even if they approve of me, they don't want the institution to continue."

She tightened her arms around him. "How do you feel?"

"I've been preparing for this for months," he said, staring out at the sea in the distance, and felt...peace. "Seeing the signs as I worked with Marabelle on the best ways to give power to the people, be it small or large. And yet now the truth is out and I feel... relieved? A little frightened. The future is...very different now."

"It will be wide open once this is done." She stepped back and took his hands. "Do you still intend to run for the position of leadership? What are you calling it?"

"Prime minister, I think they wish to call it," he said. "To lead over the elected houses of nobles and commoners, which will likely be equally split." He shook his head. "Marabelle seems to think my candidacy will be accepted. She intends to support it as leader of the uprising. It is a way to transfer power gently."

"So you will not be king, but you will still steer your country." Ophelia smiled. "And I will be by your side the entire way."

"It is the only thing that makes this bearable," he said softly, and he meant it. The transition and its chaos were not something he looked forward to, though this idea of a representative government excited him.

As did the woman at his side. So he put away the worries for a while, as he was only able to do when he held her. He pulled her close once more and dropped his lips to hers.

"Have I told you lately, my precious little hoyden, how lucky I am to have you?"

She laughed against his kiss and pushed him back into the chamber, toward their bed. "You haven't," she said. "But perhaps you might have time to show me?"

He nodded as he lowered her back on the pillows. "I have all night."

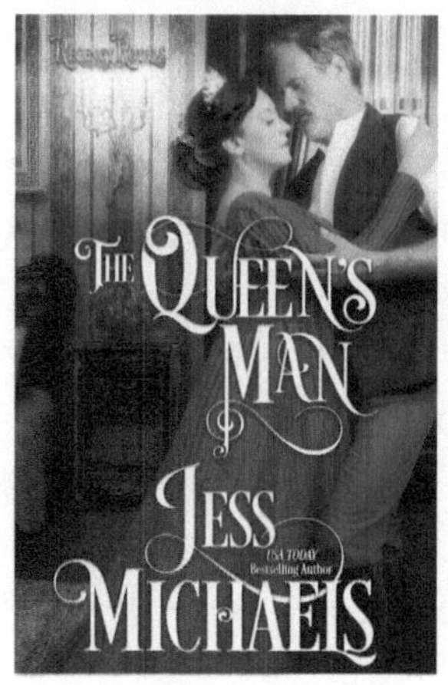

"Dashiell?"

He stopped, frozen at the sound of his name from her lips. He smoothed his jacket and slowly turned to face her. "Your Majesty, I did not realize you were still downstairs. I thought you had gone up to your quarters to have your maids ready your wardrobe."

She stepped into the hallway and closed half the distance between them. "I was going to do so, but I…I wanted to speak to you, so I waited here."

He blinked. "Speak to me?"

She motioned him toward the parlor. "Will you join me?"

He nodded and entered the room. When he turned, he watched her shut the door behind her and rest her hand against the barrier for a moment too long. They were alone. And they were often alone, yet this moment felt different somehow. More charged.

She faced him and worried her hands before her. "Have I…done something to upset you?"

He moved toward her almost against his will. "Of course not! Why would you think such a thing?"

"I could see your resistance to attending me on this trip," she said softly. "Do you not wish to go?"

"I am happy to go," he assured her. "If you saw resistance it is only because of my concerns about your safety. You know I begin to run those equations the moment a new plan is hatched."

She nodded, but there was no mistaking her relief in his answers. It washed over her beautiful face like a waterfall.

"Oh good," she breathed, raising a hand to her heart. "For you know I cannot do without you."

He moved toward her and now they were certainly too close. He flexed his fingers toward her but didn't touch her. An impossible task. "Of course, you could. You have always been more than capable at everything you've ever done Gia…" He stopped as she caught her breath. "Your Majesty," he corrected himself.

"Dash," she whispered, her voice barely carrying in the slim space between them. He saw her body coil, ready to move even closer. To go beyond too close. To unleash something he would have to physically fight to deny himself.

But before control could be lost, there was a knock on the parlor door. She jumped and stepped back before she said, "Yes?"

When the door opened, it was Giabella's maid, Betsy who stood there. Her gaze darted from the queen to Dash and back. "I'm sorry to interrupt Your Majesty, sir, but I've been informed of the imminent travel plans and I have asked that the royal tiaras and crowns be brought for you to choose from if you have time."

Giabella shot Dash a quick glance before she turned away to the door. "Yes, of course. I know we have little opportunity to ready for this journey so let us get that out of the way." She stopped and looked back over her shoulder. "Dashiell."

"Your Majesty," he said softly.

ALSO BY JESS MICHAELS

Regency Royals

To Protect a Princess

Earl's Choice

Princes are Wild

To Kiss a King

The Queen's Man (Coming Soon)

The Three Mrs

The Unexpected Wife

The Defiant Wife

The Duke's Wife

The Duke's By-Blows

The Love of a Libertine

The Heart of a Hellion

The Matter of a Marquess

The Redemption of a Rogue

The 1797 Club

The Daring Duke

Her Favorite Duke

The Broken Duke

The Silent Duke

The Duke of Nothing

The Undercover Duke

The Duke of Hearts

The Duke Who Lied

The Duke of Desire

The Last Duke

The Scandal Sheet

The Return of Lady Jane

Stealing the Duke

Lady No Says Yes

My Fair Viscount

Guarding the Countess

The House of Pleasure

Seasons

An Affair in Winter

A Spring Deception

One Summer of Surrender

Adored in Autumn

The Wicked Woodleys

Forbidden

Deceived

Tempted

Ruined

Seduced

Fascinated

To see a complete listing of Jess Michaels' titles, please visit:

http://www.authorjessmichaels.com/books

ABOUT THE AUTHOR

USA Today Bestselling author Jess Michaels likes geeky stuff, Vanilla Coke Zero, anything coconut, cheese and her dog, Elton. She is lucky enough to be married to her favorite person in the world and lives in the heart of Dallas, TX where she's trying to eat all the amazing food in the city.

When she's not obsessively checking her steps on Fitbit or trying out new flavors of Greek yogurt, she writes historical romances with smoking hot characters and emotional stories. She has written for numerous publishers and is now fully indie and loving every moment of it (well, almost every moment).

Jess loves to hear from fans! So please feel free to contact her at Jess@AuthorJessMichaels.com.

Jess Michaels offers a free book to members of her newsletter, so sign up on her website:
http://www.AuthorJessMichaels.com/

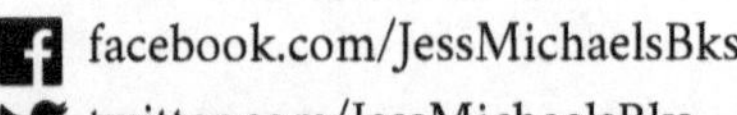

facebook.com/JessMichaelsBks
twitter.com/JessMichaelsBks
instagram.com/JessMichaelsBks
bookbub.com/authors/jess-michaels

www.ingramcontent.com/pod-product-compliance
Lightning Source LLC
Chambersburg PA
CBHW050851190726
48286CB00007B/2335